More
Fifth Grade
Magic

MAY

More Fifth Grade Magic

by Beatrice Gormley

illustrated by Emily Arnold McCully

E. P. DUTTON   NEW YORK

Library of Congress Cataloging-in-Publication Data

Gormley, Beatrice.
  More fifth grade magic.

  Summary: Wishing she could be more assertive with
her domineering mother, fifth grader and professional
model Amy Sacher finds a magic calendar that can change
her life. Sequel to "Fifth Grade Magic."
  [1. Magic—Fiction. 2. Mothers and daughters—
Fiction. 3. Assertiveness (Psychology)—Fiction.
4. Models, Fashion—Fiction.] I. McCully, Emily Arnold,
ill. II. Title.
PZ7.G6696Mo 1989 [Fic] 88-25683
ISBN 0-525-44486-6

Published in the United States by
E. P. Dutton, a division of
Penguin Books USA Inc.

Published simultaneously in Canada by
Fitzhenry & Whiteside Limited, Toronto

Editor: Ann Durell

Printed in the U.S.A.   First Edition
10 9 8 7 6 5 4 3 2 1

to Mitzi, my oldest friend

Contents

1

You Won't Believe Me

Amy had a plan. She stepped out of the cafeteria line and looked across the crowded lunch room, wondering if it was a good idea after all.

She had thought of it that morning, as soon as she realized Kathy was out sick. Kathy was the girl who had glommed onto Amy when she moved to Rushfield a few months ago. But the most interesting girl in Amy's class, the girl Amy really wanted to get to know, was Gretchen.

Squinting toward the table where the girls in Mrs. Sheppard's class always sat, Amy saw that Gretchen was sitting in her usual place, near one end. And there was no one on that side of her. Good. If Kathy were here, she would make a fuss about Amy's sitting down next to Gretchen, but today maybe Amy could do it as if it were no big deal.

But suppose Gretchen acted unfriendly, the way she had been until last week, after the play . . .

1

Someone bumped into Amy from behind. "Make up your mind!"

Go, Amy told herself. Quickly she made what she called a "magic bargain": If you can get to that table without touching anybody, Gretchen will be friendly.

Amy began to weave her way among the noisy tables as if she were playing soccer with a tray in her hands. That boy was leaning way out from the bench . . . another boy flung an arm in Amy's path, and she dodged just in time . . . that girl was sticking her leg right in front of Amy, so she had to give a little hop at the last minute, and her fruit cup slopped onto her tray.

But Amy had gotten through without touching anyone, and here she was—on the bench next to Gretchen.

Gretchen glanced at Amy's tray. "You didn't get any brownies."

"They must have run out," said Amy shyly. "I'm not really supposed to eat chocolate, anyway."

"Oh, come on," said Gretchen. She bent her brownie until it broke, and placed one half on Amy's tray. "Live a little!"

"So what happens if you do eat chocolate?" Beth leaned across Gretchen, toward Amy. "Do you get a bunch of pimples, just like regular kids who aren't models?"

Amy winced. She knew how Beth, and a lot of the kids in her class, felt about her—that she was conceited and standoffish because she was a professional model.

But Gretchen grinned in a friendly way. "Hey, wouldn't it be funny if you just took one bite of that brownie and, *boing,* pimples popped out all over your face?"

2

In the middle of sipping her milk, Amy giggled and sputtered.

"Yeah," said Beth without laughing. "That'd be the end of your great career."

"You sound like my mother." Amy sighed.

"Speaking of mothers," said Gretchen, turning to Beth, "did you ask her if you could sign up for Young Theater?"

Beth nodded. "It's okay."

"What's Young Theater?" Amy couldn't help asking.

"It's a Recreation Department program," explained Gretchen. "For the summer. I've been in it every year. But this will be the best year, because they give the main parts to the fifth graders, since we'll be too old for Young Theater next summer. You should sign up, too."

"I think I could." Amy tried to keep her tone casual. This was like a wish come true. A wish that she hadn't even dared to make. "I'm going to the Delaware shore for two weeks with my father, but that isn't until the end of the summer. Where do you sign up?"

"At the high school gym, on Saturday," said Gretchen with a pleased expression. "Better get there early. Sometimes the good classes fill up."

"Yeah, like the foursquare line, if we don't hurry." Popping the last bite of her sandwich into her mouth, Beth stood up. "I'm going to the rest room before there's two million first graders in there."

This was turning out so much better than Amy had even imagined. Now she had a chance to talk with Gretchen alone. There was something she very much wanted to ask her. She just hoped it wouldn't make Gretchen mad and spoil everything. She took a deep breath. "Er—you know that time—that weird day, a while ago . . . ?"

Gretchen's freckled face stiffened, and she poked a crust on her plate. "What time?"

It had been *such* a weird day that it was hard for Amy to put into words what had happened. "You know. We changed places." She shuddered, remembering the shock. First waking up in a strange bed, and then looking in the mirror to see Gretchen's freckles and wavy ginger-colored hair. "You were me, and I was . . . you."

"Yeah." A long pause. "I'm sorry." Gretchen squinted down her straw, as if she might find an excuse there for what she had done. "I should have asked you first, but I didn't get a chance. If you really want to know, I thought you probably wouldn't want to exchange."

Amy leaned closer. "I'm not mad at you. I just wondered, how did you do it?"

"I didn't, exactly." Gretchen spoke slowly. "Someone else did."

"Well, who was it?" Amy's heart beat faster. At last Gretchen was going to let her in on her incredible secret.

"You won't believe me, if I tell you." Gretchen crushed the crust with her thumb. Her mouth worked, as if she was trying to say something that wouldn't come out. Finally she gave a deep sigh. "It was my fairy godmother."

Amy stared. Then she gave a disbelieving laugh. Was Gretchen making fun of her? She drew back.

"I knew you wouldn't believe me," said Gretchen. Her face was as red as a freckled tomato.

Amy didn't know what to think. She was about to ask

4

Gretchen what she meant by a fairy godmother when Beth plopped down on the bench across from them. "Boy, aren't you through yet? We have to line up for foursquare."

"Oh, yeah!" Gretchen jumped up, looking relieved. "Come on, Amy. You can eat the brownie on the playground."

Walking home that afternoon, Amy was still wondering what Gretchen had meant. She couldn't believe that Gretchen was teasing her. Gretchen didn't seem like the kind of person who would make something up just to tease Amy. Gretchen said what she thought and didn't try to hide the way she felt—that had gotten her into trouble with the teacher a couple of times.

So if Gretchen had decided she liked Amy, why wouldn't she tell her how they had switched places? Amy couldn't figure it out. But she was sure of one thing: Gretchen wouldn't have shared her brownie with Amy if she didn't like her. Now that they were going to spend the whole summer together in Young Theater, who knows—they might get to be good friends.

If Mother would let her sign up. Amy glanced at her watch. It was 3:05. Usually it took Amy fifteen minutes to walk home, but if she ran, she could probably get there in ten minutes. If I get home by 3:15, she bargained with herself, Mother will let me sign up for Young Theater.

Amy had never really had a good friend, at least not for the last few years. Ever since Mother and Daddy had gotten divorced, she had moved around a lot. First to the city, then to a town near the city, and finally to Rushfield, where a lot of people were building houses and Mother thought there would be more "scope" for her interior design business.

Amy's side ached. She was used to running, but not with a heavy book bag. Still, she forced herself to run on, past all the white two-story houses with small-paned windows. The houses in this part of Rushfield had been built two hundred years ago, or looked as if they had.

Gasping as she stopped by her own mailbox, Amy glanced at her watch. Three twelve—she had made it. She put her hands on her knees for a moment, to catch her breath.

The house Amy's mother had bought was new, and looked it. The front of the house was blank rectangles of unpainted boards, and the second-story roof slanted off at an unexpected angle. "Oh, you live in that weird house on Mallard Street," a girl had said to Amy when they first moved here.

Of course every time they moved, Amy had to start over at a new school with new kids. She never got to feel comfortable anywhere. It was as if she always had to wear the stiff, chemical-smelling new clothes she modeled and never got to put on her nice soft old sweat suit.

But now, thought Amy as she passed her mother's silver Audi in the garage, now things might be different. If she could take Young Theater with the other girls, she might actually get to feeling comfortable here. Let's see, if the sign-up was Saturday, and this was Tuesday, that would give her mother four days to plan.

Mother liked to know about things ahead of time and write them down on her calendar. If Amy asked her at the last minute if she could stay overnight with someone or if Mother would take Amy to the video store to rent a movie, Mother's eyebrows would draw together. "I need to have a little advance warning, angel. My schedule is so tight, between building up my business and running *your* career, to say nothing of keeping fit. . . ."

In the high-ceilinged, gleaming white kitchen Amy set her book bag down on a counter. Water was running upstairs, so her mother must be taking a shower. Good. That would give Amy a chance to get ready before she talked to her.

Looking around the kitchen for something helpful to do, Amy discovered that the dishwasher was full of clean dishes. She put them away. Then she clattered up the circular iron staircase to her bedroom, unpinned her calendar from the wall, and sat down at her desk.

At the beginning of the year her mother had given her the calendar and urged her to write down all her appointments, but somehow Amy had never gotten around to it. In fact, the calendar looked so uninteresting that she had never even turned the pages past January.

"A Year's Journey" was the title of the calendar. The first picture showed a girl in a long, old-fashioned dress, with little black shoes like ballet slippers peeping out from underneath her skirt. You couldn't see the girl's face, since she was turned sideways and the hood of her long cloak was pulled over her head. Carrying a basket on one arm, she was walking along a road that wound over hills and through valleys. "The Romantic style of the calendar makes a nice contrast with your Swedish modern furniture," Mother had said.

"Tra-la, tra-la," said Amy scornfully to the sweet and dainty-looking girl on the calendar. She would rather have had a cat calendar, but it was never any use saying anything.

Flipping the pages, Amy paused to look at the picture for March. It showed the same cloaked and hooded girl. But now the path led directly into a dark forest. The girl looked tiny, compared to the towering trees.

Amy felt a tingle of excitement. Somehow the picture made her think of that weird day in March when she had traded places with Gretchen.

Then Amy looked up from the calendar, aware that the sounds in the house had changed. Uh-oh. The running water had stopped, which meant her mother was out of the shower. Amy had better get on with writing down "commitments," as her mother called them, on the calendar.

Quickly Amy turned the page to May—and paused again. Now the cloaked girl had come to a clearing deep in the forest. Huge branches arched over the space, shutting out most of the light, but Amy could make out tree trunks like pillars around a pool.

The person in the cloak looked different in this picture. Amy wasn't sure what made the difference, but now she looked more mysterious than sweet or dainty.

Pulling her eyes away from the picture, Amy focused on the ruled-off dates below it. In the space for Saturday she wrote in pencil, *Go to high school gym. Sign up for Y.T.*

"Hello, angel."

Amy turned to see her mother, her hair wrapped in a towel-turban, standing in the doorway. "Hi, Mother. I was just writing down my commitments on my calendar."

An approving smile spread over Mrs. Sacher's face. She crossed the room and sat on the edge of Amy's desk.

Amy smelled the scent of her mother's shampoo and felt the brush of her silky dressing gown.

"Very good, Amy! I'm glad you've realized how important it is to use your calendar." There was a pause, and then she asked, "What is this about Y.T. on Saturday?"

"Young Theater," said Amy, trying to hold her breath and talk at the same time. "It's a summer program. I have to sign up Saturday morning. Gret—" Amy remembered in time that her mother thought Gretchen was aggressive and uncontrolled. "The kids say the director is wonderful, and we'll learn a lot about acting."

Her mother nodded as if she wasn't really listening. "That sounds like a nice thing to do, if you were going to stay in Rushfield this summer. But I have a thrilling surprise for you." The corners of her mouth twitched with excitement. "Do you remember, this winter, I looked into a summer camp for you, a modeling camp? Camp KidShine. But then your father and I decided it was too expensive."

Amy's heart sank. "Yes."

"But now my business is starting to take off—I may even get the chance to decorate the Trenton house, that fabulous contemporary. And your father is better off financially, too, although he doesn't like to admit it. So I called the KidShine director this morning, and would you believe it, they just had a cancellation!" She beamed at her daughter. "So come June 29, you'll be off to the Catskills for six weeks."

2

I Need Magic

Off to the Catskills for six weeks. To Amy it sounded like a prison sentence. "But I wanted to stay here this summer. With the kids I know. We were going to have a good time."

"A good time!" Mrs. Sacher laughed indulgently. "I can't tell you how many *good times* I've given up to get my career on the fast track. That's the trade-off a professional person has to make."

Amy's mind darted this way and that, like a frantic chipmunk in the middle of the road. "Well, then, why do I have to go for the whole six weeks?" she asked. "Maybe I could be in Young Theater half the summer and go to camp for the other half."

Under the towel-turban, Mrs. Sacher's brows drew together. "Angel, do you understand what an opportunity this is? You'll be learning techniques from top professional models, working with top fashion photographers. This modeling for catalogues you've been doing is all right to start with, but there's a lot more than that in *your* future."

"Maybe I won't get in," suggested Amy in desperation. "They have to choose you, don't they?"

"They admitted you last winter," said her mother. "I didn't tell you then, because I thought you couldn't go anyway, but the director liked your portfolio."

Amy looked up into her mother's glowing face and tried to think about how thrilling it was. But all she could think of was Gretchen and Beth at Young Theater together, comfortable and chummy.

"Now, let's get back to your calendar," Mrs. Sacher went on. "You know, it may be hard to believe, but it's true: If you'll just write things down on your calendar, you can actually take control of your life."

You mean, *you* can take control of my life, thought Amy, with anger that surprised her. I ran all the way home for nothing. I put away the dishes for nothing.

"First of all, erase that entry for Saturday, since you won't be signing up for the theater program." As Amy slowly picked up her pencil and erased what she had written, her mother added, "Saturday might be a good time to shop for your camp clothes."

Amy said nothing, staring down at the picture on her calendar. The cloaked girl knelt on the far side of the pool, facing Amy but with her head bowed so that the hood fell over her face. Her spread hands, palms up, seemed to offer the dark, still pool to Amy like a crystal ball.

I know what my future is, thank you, Amy thought. And I hate it.

Slipping from Amy's desk, Mrs. Sacher said, "I'd better go dry my hair, but I couldn't wait to tell you the good news. Be sure to write down your appointment with the photographer tomorrow, angel," she added from the doorway. "That's at four o'clock."

Anger seethed to the top of Amy's head like soda spurting out of a shaken-up can. As soon as her mother was gone, Amy grabbed a purple felt pen from her pencil holder. She scrawled in the space for tomorrow, Wednesday: *Mother's little angel to photographer.*

Writing the last word slowed Amy down, and she giggled nervously. But she didn't erase the purple scrawl.

Glancing at the calendar picture again, Amy noticed that the glassy surface of the pool seemed to quiver, as if something had dropped into it. Strange, the way some pictures looked like they were moving.

Amy sighed and put down the pen. If only . . . If only, what? It was hard even to imagine what wonderful thing might happen so that she could take Young Theater after all. What *impossible* thing. Anything Amy could think of that would keep her from going to camp, like breaking a leg, would keep her from going to the theater program, too.

Something impossible, thought Amy. That's what I need.

A funny feeling came over her, as if the world turned upside down for a moment. On one weird day, she remembered, something impossible *had* happened. That day she found herself in Gretchen's body.

"It was my fairy godmother," Gretchen had said.

What happened that day wasn't like Amy's magic bargain that if she didn't touch anyone in the cafeteria, Gretchen would be friendly. No—on that day in March, there had been *real* magic at work.

Her lungs filling with a frightening hope, Amy jumped up from her desk and hurried downstairs to the phone in the kitchen.

Gretchen answered right away. "Hello."

"Hi, it's Amy."

"Oh, hi."

"Hi." Amy paused, biting her lip. She didn't know exactly what to say.

"Well, hi-hi-hi!" Gretchen laughed. "Amy, what did you call me up for?"

"Um . . . remember what you told me at lunch?"

"You mean about Young Theater?"

"Um . . . no." Amy felt her face growing warm, and she dropped her voice. "About the—about your fairy godmother."

There was a silence, during which Amy wondered if she had gone crazy and imagined the whole thing. Then Gretchen said in a guarded tone, "Yeah?"

Amy's breath grew shallow, making it harder to talk. "I just wanted to ask you, that was a joke, right? About your—um—f.g. making things happen?"

"Why are you asking me again?" Gretchen sounded suspicious. "If I was going to make up a story, I'd make up a better one than that. Like aliens from a U.F.O., or a crazy scientist with a weird invention."

"I guess so," said Amy. She paused, then blurted out, "How did you find her?"

"Why do you want to know?" Now Gretchen sounded alarmed. "I hope you don't think it would be a good idea to call for *your* f.g. and make some wishes, because it would *not*! Don't you remember what an awful fix we got into?"

Amy remembered some embarrassing things, all right, like screaming at Gretchen to get out of her body, and like Mrs. Sheppard hauling her off to the principal. But the main thing she remembered was how exciting it had been. That day was something Amy's mother had not written down on her calendar. "Yes, but didn't it turn out all right for you, in the end?" In a choked whisper she added, "I need magic."

"No, you don't!" Gretchen sighed loudly. "Believe me, magic just gets you in a terrible mess, and I'm not going to tell you how to do it, so stop asking me."

Gretchen was going to hang up. Amy squeezed the receiver in both hands, as if she could keep her on the phone that way. "But can't you just tell me how your f.g.—"

"Don't tie up the phone, angel." Mrs. Sacher appeared at the end of the counter, her hair now dry and perfectly styled. "I need to make some business calls."

Amy said good-bye and hung up, her eyes smarting with forced-back tears. How could Gretchen be that mean?

Opening her business notebook, her mother took over the stool by the phone. "Who were you talking to, angel? And what does f.g. mean?"

It means mind your own business, thought Amy. Aloud she muttered, "Just a girl from school. She's the one who kept saying f.g. I guess it's a swearword."

Mrs. Sacher looked mystified, but her attention was on the number she was tapping into the phone. "Oh. You don't want to hang around with girls who use vulgar language. Go get your sweat suit on, and we'll go running right after I make these calls."

That evening Amy had a headache. "Like a steel band squeezing your head?" asked her mother sympathetically. She held out a Tylenol pill and a glass of water.

"Not exactly." Amy tried to think what it was like. "More like something trying to pop *out,* all around my head." Seeing the horror on her mother's face, she realized that sounded like pimples. She added quickly, "I guess it *is* like a steel band."

"Pop out?" Mrs. Sacher brushed back Amy's bangs and peered at her face. "I don't see any spots." Then she drew back, her eyes narrowing. "I think maybe you have a guilty conscience. Tell Mother the truth—have you been eating chocolate? *The day before a modeling appointment?"*

Then Amy had to listen to a lecture she had heard before, the one about how nothing was more important than taking care of her skin, and how the enjoyment of eating chocolate only lasted a few moments, but the satisfaction of a successful career lasted a lifetime. If her mother had lost her voice, Amy could give the lecture to herself.

Going off to bed at last, Amy wondered if one little half-brownie could have made her head feel so funny. After all, when she ate chocolate at Daddy's nothing bad ever happened to her skin.

In the middle of the night Amy half woke up. There's a light on, she thought groggily.

She squinted at the lamp on her desk, across the room, at the track lights on the ceiling. They were all dark. And yet, a faint glow was coming from somewhere.

Who cares, thought Amy as she pulled up the covers and drifted back into sleep. It's not my problem.

Across the room, the dark pool in the calendar picture reflected an eerie light.

When Amy got up the next morning, she thought she heard a faint humming, like the sound her desk lamp made. But she wasn't sitting at her desk, and besides, the lamp was off. Probably her ears were still clogged from the cold she had had last week.

In the bathroom Amy picked up the washcloth and looked into the mirror. She frowned and blinked. There must be something wrong with the lights around the mirror, because it looked as if a ring of light was shining from her head. With a laugh at that idea, Amy switched off the bathroom lights.

But light still seemed to be shining out of her head. In fact, it was clearer now that the bathroom lights were off. The light formed a flat circle, like one of the rings of Saturn.

Was something going wrong with her eyes? Amy glanced anxiously around the bathroom. But the scale on the floor, the bright pattern on the shower curtain, and her toothbrush hanging from the toothbrush holder all looked normal.

Amy gave another laugh, a nervous one, and rubbed

her scalp hard. *There*—when she pressed on a place where the circle of golden light met her head, that turned it off. But now it made a buzzing noise, and her hand tingled.

Amy took her hand away from her head. The circle of light popped out again.

A rap on the bathroom door made Amy jump. "Angel," called her mother's voice, "I want to say something to you."

3

A Minor Defect

Amy glanced at the mirror again, at her open mouth and staring eyes, and especially at the disk of light shimmering around her blonde head. She couldn't let Mother see her looking like a planet with a ring around it—she would have a fit.

Grabbing a towel from the rack, Amy wrapped it into a turban, the way her mother did when she got out of the shower. Then she opened the door.

"Oh, you did take a shower. I didn't hear the water running." Mrs. Sacher didn't seem to notice anything strange. "I was just going to remind you to wash your hair, since you're seeing the photographer this afternoon."

"I remembered," said Amy, feeling a twinge of guilt.

"Yes, because you wrote it down on your calendar," said her mother. "I knew that would help, angel."

Back in her room, Amy stared into the full-length mirror on the door, letting the towel drop to her shoulders. The ring of light shone out around her head.

Seized with a fit of giggles, she pressed her hand to her mouth. What's so funny? she scolded herself. You'd better get dressed.

And she couldn't wear a towel on her head to school. Maybe her headband . . . Yes, if she pulled the headband exactly over the . . . the *thing,* it shut off. It made the humming turn into a buzz, but she would just have to put up with that.

After getting dressed, Amy went downstairs for breakfast. In the kitchen her mother was sitting at the counter, drinking coffee and reading the business section of the paper. She looked up and smiled as she saw Amy, but the smile quickly turned into a frown. "You aren't planning to wear *that* today, I hope."

Amy looked down at her belted jump suit in astonishment. "Why not? This is what you laid out for me to wear."

"Not the jump suit." Her mother made an impatient gesture. "That grubby old headband. Remember, you're going to the photographer right after school."

Putting both hands on the headband, as if her mother might rip it off, Amy tried to think of an argument. "What does it matter what I wear to the photographer? I have to change when I get there, anyway."

Mrs. Sacher shook her head and sighed. "Angel, I thought you understood, by now, how important it is to make a good impression on everyone you work with. You can't afford to show up at the photographer's looking half put-together."

"All right, all right." Amy ran back up the stairs to her

room. She didn't know what she was going to do when she got there, but it was easier to think away from her mother.

Maybe there was something else she could wear on her head, something better than a headband. . . . Something like . . . that floppy felt hat Mother had bought for her last audition! It was the same color as her jump suit!

Amy took the hat from her closet and settled it on her head. There. It shut off the light, and it looked put-to-gether—at least, Amy thought so.

When she came downstairs the second time, Mrs. Sacher nodded and smiled. "Very nice choice! But do you think you should wear a hat to school? I could bring it along when I pick you up this afternoon. Don't they have a rule against wearing hats in class?"

"I'm not sure," said Amy, although she *was* pretty sure there was a rule like that. She pulled the brim of the hat more firmly over her forehead, ignoring the buzzing noise. "I really want to wear it today. Maybe Mrs. Sheppard won't say anything."

Mrs. Sacher laughed knowingly. "She has a soft spot for you, doesn't she? Well, of course she does—my angel's so pretty and sweet."

By the time she got to school, Amy wished that she had taken the time to do something (but what?) about the ring of light around her head. It didn't seem to like being kept down by the hat, and it buzzed against her skull.

In the classroom Amy saw the heads turning toward her and her felt hat, but she ignored them and sat down in her seat next to Kathy.

"What a great hat," said Kathy. "Is that the one you wore for your last audition?"

Amy nodded. "I'm going to a photographer after school today." She didn't say that was why she was wearing the hat, but she would let Kathy think that.

"Guess what I did yesterday when I was home sick?" Kathy pulled a piece of lined paper from her current events folder. "I made a list of all the celebrities I know. I know seven!"

"Really?" To Amy, Kathy's voice seemed to add to the buzzing around her head, but she took the list politely. Kathy had stuck gold and red stars around the top of the paper. "Are you sure they're all famous? I never heard of Manny Olsen."

"Okay, I'll explain." Kathy leaned over and pointed. "Manny Olsen is my second cousin—he was on a game show. And—"

"Wait a minute. You put *me* on the list!" Amy had spotted her own name, with gold stars before and after it. "I'm not a celebrity."

"Your picture was in the paper, wasn't it? Uh-oh." Kathy glanced toward the teacher out of the corner of her eye. "I'd better put my list away."

But Amy had already noticed the way Mrs. Sheppard was pushing up her pink-lensed glasses at her, and she didn't think the teacher's frown was for the paper Kathy slid back in her folder. Sure enough, Mrs. Sheppard got up from her desk, walked over, and bent down to whisper to Amy. "Don't you think you'd be more comfortable if you hung your hat in the closet, dear?"

"Oh, I can't," said Amy. Gazing with wide eyes from under the brim, she held on to it with both hands. "Please, Mrs. Sheppard, can't I wear it? Just today?"

"Amy needs her hat for modeling." Kathy spoke up

importantly. "She's going to the photographer's after school."

The teacher straightened, looking undecided. She fingered one of her large pearl earrings. "But I don't see why . . ."

A swell of laughter on the other side of the classroom made Mrs. Sheppard turn to look. Dennis Boyd, the class clown, was sitting at his desk with his hands folded, looking straight ahead. He was wearing his Red Sox cap.

"Dennis," said Mrs. Sheppard sharply. "I thought you understood from our talk yesterday morning that we don't wear . . ." She looked back at Amy in her floppy felt hat.

"I thought today must be National Hat Day." Dennis gave the teacher one of his fake-angelic smiles. His friends laughed.

Mrs. Sheppard's frown deepened, and Amy was sure the teacher was going to make them both take off their hats. She thought of what her mother often told her clients: "A new light fixture can transform a room." Room 5A would be transformed, all right.

But Mrs. Sheppard only pressed her lips together and went back to her attendance book.

Kathy nudged Amy and smirked, as if to say, "She'll do anything you want." Amy looked away.

"Teacher's pet wins again." That was Beth's loud whisper from the back of the room.

Amy wanted to shout to the whole class: "Do you think I like being a teacher's pet?" But of course that was just what they did think.

During reading groups, when the teacher's back was turned, Dennis sneaked up to the chalkboard and drew a heart and wrote *Mrs. S. + Amy* in it. As soon as the kids started laughing, Mrs. Sheppard turned around and made Dennis erase it. But Amy wondered if one of those unfriendly snickers was Gretchen's.

What was almost worse, at lunch Kathy blabbed to everyone that Amy was modeling this afternoon. Several kids wanted to know what it was like, and if she made a lot of money, and if she was going to be in the movies pretty soon. All the questions seemed to buzz around Amy, the way the hidden shining circle buzzed against her head, until she wanted to scream.

The only good thing that happened that day was the note, a piece of lined paper folded and taped shut, that Amy found on her desk after recess.

AMY—PRIVATE!!! was printed on the outside. Amy was afraid it might be a mean note about her being a teacher's pet. But the bold, forward-slanting writing inside said, *I'm sorry I yelled at you yesterday. Don't be mad! F.g.'s are bad news and I know what I'm talking about. G.N.*

Noticing Kathy craning her neck to read the note, Amy folded it up and slipped it into her pocket.

When three o'clock came, Amy was glad to run out of school and jump into her mother's waiting Audi.

"Off to work we go!" Mrs. Sacher was in good spirits.

Amy fastened her seat belt and sank back with a sigh. But then the thought of where they were going made her jerk upright. Wait a minute! she thought. I must be crazy. When I get to the photographer's, they'll make me take off the hat.

Glancing at her mother from the corner of her eye, Amy said brightly, "I just love this hat you bought me. I

25

should get some more use out of it, since it cost so much. I sure hope the photographer will let me wear it today."

Through her sunglasses Mrs. Sacher gave Amy a puzzled frown. "You weren't paying attention, angel. This is a Christmas toy catalogue, and you're supposed to wear winter play clothes, remember? I brought a ski hat for you."

"Oh, that's right," said Amy. She leaned back in her seat, as if she could slow the car down. Maybe the ring of light would just disappear any minute, the way it had come. If I bite my tongue the whole way, she bargained with herself, the light will turn off. But the light kept on buzzing under her hat, like a trapped fly.

"Headache all gone?" asked her mother.

Amy hesitated. As a matter of fact, her head didn't feel too wonderful after being buzzed all day. Maybe she should try to get out of modeling by playing sick.

But no—if Mother thought Amy was sick, she would be sure to take her hat off to feel her forehead. "Unhuh," she said, still holding her tongue firmly with her teeth. No, her best hope was to go to the photo session. Maybe she could whip off her felt hat and jam on the ski hat before anyone noticed her light fixture.

The photographer, a bearded man, opened the door of his studio. "Sacher, right?" He glanced at a schedule on his desk, then nodded toward a screen in the corner. "You can change back there."

Behind the screen, Amy watched closely as her mother pulled a turtleneck jersey and bibbed ski pants out of the bag. Amy grabbed a snowflake-pattern ski hat by its pompom, murmuring, "I'll just put this on first."

"What?" Mrs. Sacher put one hand on her hip. "Don't

start fooling around now. Take off your hat and jump suit and put on the jersey."

Oh, no. Grabbing the brim of her hat with both hands, Amy looked around the cubicle wildly for a way to escape. "I can't."

"Come on, angel. You're a professional, so start acting like one." Mrs. Sacher reached out to take the hat.

Amy backed up, but there was nowhere to back. Leaning away from her mother's hands, she stumbled against the screen—and kept going.

There was a resounding crash. Her mother screamed. Amy lay flat on top of the screen, with the breath knocked out of her.

"Hey, watch that, there!" The photographer, adjusting some lights on poles, looked annoyed. "You could have knocked over a camera."

"A camera!" exclaimed Mrs. Sacher angrily, bending over her daughter. "Angel, are you all right?"

"I . . . think so," gasped Amy, putting her hands to her head. But she already knew, because the buzzing had stopped, that her hat must have fallen off.

Her mother's expression of alarm changed to puzzlement. Still staring down at Amy, she blinked her eyes the way Amy had when she'd looked in the mirror this morning. Somehow the sight of her mother looking so baffled struck Amy funny, and she started giggling.

"I'm all set here," said the photographer, picking up the fallen screen. "There's another appointment scheduled for five, so if you'll just get your kid to turn off her halo, and get her into the winter clothes. . . ."

Turn off her halo! That struck Amy even funnier. She tried to get up, but she was laughing too hard.

"Amy Renata Sacher," said her mother in a dangerous voice. "Where did you get that thing?" She yanked Amy to her feet, seized her head in both hands, and peered at her hair. Like a mother monkey, thought Amy, trying to choke back her giggles.

In a rising tone Mrs. Sacher went on, "Did that Gretchen Nichols have anything to do with this? How do you get it off?"

The photographer peered over her shoulder. "Amazing, what they can do with miniaturization. I can't even see the wires for the light." He added briskly, "But let's go—we should have started working five minutes ago."

"Ow!" Amy tried to pull away from her mother, who was pawing frantically through her hair. "Don't! It doesn't come off."

"Hey, can we stop fooling around here?" Now the photographer looked annoyed. "The modeling agency told me this kid was very cooperative. Are we going to shoot pictures, or what?"

Letting go of Amy, Mrs. Sacher swallowed and licked her lips. "Well. Nobody expected this, but I think the obvious thing is just to go on with the session. Amy, let's pop your winter clothes on, and—"

"Go on with the session!" The photographer laughed disbelievingly. "With a halo on her head?"

"Why not?" said Mrs. Sacher. "It's a Christmas catalogue, isn't it?"

"You must have lost it, lady. Playtime Toys told me straight shots, no gimmicks."

Mrs. Sacher's mouth twitched in a smile. "All right, but it's really only a minor defect. You could airbrush it out."

He laughed again, not in a nice way. "I've seen pushy

29

mothers, but you really win the prize. Airbrush it! You think I'm going to do all that extra work because your kid insists on wearing her halo? That's your problem." He stepped to his desk and picked up the phone.

"What are you doing?" Mrs. Sacher grabbed his arm.

But he shook her off. "I'm calling the agency to tell them to send another model."

Mrs. Sacher tried to argue some more, but it was no use. She and Amy had to stuff the winter clothes back in the bag and leave the studio. Amy wasn't laughing anymore—she knew that when her mother got that upset, life was not going to be very pleasant for Amy. There was only one good thing: Now that the hat was off, the buzzing against her head wasn't bothering her.

They rode home in terrible silence. Once or twice Amy started to say, "Really, it wasn't my idea" or "It just happened overnight." But then she shut her mouth. Feeble excuses would only make Mother more angry.

When they were in the house, Amy expected her mother to examine her head again, but Mrs. Sacher went straight for the phone. "First thing is to sweet-talk the agency," she said grimly. Then, after someone spoke on the other end of the line, her voice turned bright and businesslike. "I called to apologize for the mix-up this afternoon. You see, Amy was victimized by some problem children at school."

Amy knew her mother was just making up an excuse to tell the modeling agency, but she wondered. *Had* one of the kids at school done this to her? With a voodoo doll or something? Amy knew kids who would enjoy playing a mean trick on her, but she didn't think this was the

30

right kind of trick for them. They would be more likely to give her a potato for a nose.

"And so when we arrived at the photographer's," Mrs. Sacher went on, "she had lights on her scalp." She paused to listen. Then she said sharply, "No. Not lice. Lights. L-i-g-h-t-s."

Amy didn't especially want to stick around, because it seemed that her mother would be madder than ever by the time she got off the phone. But when she tried to slip away, her mother frowned and pointed to the kitchen floor, as if to say, *"Stay."*

After she finished explaining to the agency, Mrs. Sacher called a doctor who treated diseases of the scalp. This time she didn't mention the lights. She scribbled on a note pad, said, "Fine. Tomorrow at ten o'clock," and hung up. She turned to Amy.

Amy was used to her mother's gazing at her with satisfied admiration, as though she were looking in a mirror, but now Mrs. Sacher looked past Amy's shoulder as she spoke. "All right. Put this on your calendar: tomorrow at ten, to dermatologist. You'll just have to miss school—this is much more important."

Glad to escape to her room, Amy hurried up the stairs. She unpinned her calendar from the wall and put one knee on her desk chair. Let's see, tomorrow was Thursday.

Running along the rows of squares, her gaze came to a halt on today's date. There in the square for Wednesday, May 11, was her purple scrawl: *Mother's little angel to photographer.*

Angel. Halo. *Oh.*

31

Amy's mouth dropped open. She put a hand up to the humming circle on her head. She shifted her gaze to the picture on the calendar.

There was the hooded figure, still kneeling beside the dark pool in the forest. Under the surface of the mysterious pool glimmered a flat golden circle.

4

Amy Takes Control

For a moment Amy just sat there, trying to take it in. She had written on the calendar that Mother's little angel would go to the photographer's this afternoon. *That was what had happened.* Not the way she had meant it, exactly, but the way she wrote it.

"Hee! Hee!" Wild laughter bubbled out of Amy. She jumped up from her desk and began to dance in front of the mirror, flapping her arms like wings. I made this happen! she thought.

But how? Calming down, Amy went back to her desk and picked up the purple felt pen. She squinted at it, turning it over. She had written lots of things with this pen, and nothing weird had happened before.

But she had never written on the *calendar* before yesterday. Amy's glance moved to the picture. The cloaked figure with the unseen face bent over the pool. Like a crystal ball, Amy remembered. To see my future.

The eerie quiet of that clearing in the forest surrounded Amy, and she felt again a tingle of the excitement she had felt when she and Gretchen changed places. Then she remembered what she had said to Gretchen yesterday: "I need magic."

Her heart began to trip. Had she gotten what she asked for? Not a fairy godmother, but something just as good.

Impossible. It was impossible that something had happened because she wrote it down on her calendar, no matter how magical the calendar picture looked.

Then why was she wearing a halo?

Well, go ahead and test the magic, Amy told herself. See what happens. The first thing to try was getting rid of the silly halo. She could write—no, maybe she could just erase.

Even with an ink eraser, it took Amy a while to rub the felt pen letters off of the calendar. But as soon as the last bit of purple rolled off the page in eraser crumbs, Gretchen felt a sharp crackling around her head, like a worn light bulb going out.

Amy rushed to the mirror on the door. Gone! The halo was gone! It worked! Now she knew how to handle the magic of the calendar.

Grinning at herself in the mirror, Amy thought, I like the way I look. Daddy always said that she got the best of both sides of the family: her mother's good looks and her father's good nature. But right now, for the first time, Amy thought she just looked like herself. She remembered something her mother had said yesterday afternoon, something about using a calendar to take control of your life.

Amy narrowed her eyes thoughtfully as she walked back to the desk. Oh, yes, she thought. This calendar certainly will help me take control. And I know the first thing I'm going to do. I'm going to fix it so that I'll stay in Rushfield and be in Young Theater this summer.

No, just a minute. She should be more careful. Gretchen had warned her. "Magic just gets you in a terrible mess." Of course Gretchen didn't know about calendar magic. Still, Amy should be careful. Before she started writing down what she really wanted to happen, she should try a little experiment.

Tina, an older model Amy had worked with, had given her advice like that about new makeup. "Don't put it right on your face—it might make you break out. Try a little patch on skin that doesn't show, like the underside of your arm." So Amy would write down something simple and harmless, write down that it would happen a few minutes from now.

Amy turned to glance at the clock beside her bed. Five forty-nine. Okay, she would write on the calendar that at exactly six o'clock, someone would call her. Not Kathy or Daddy or anyone else who usually called, but—

Amy giggled out loud as a bold idea struck her. The president. If the president called up Amy Sacher, she would know for sure that she could work magic with the calendar.

On the calendar the square for today was mostly thin and rough where Amy had erased the purple scrawl about going to the photographer. But there was enough smooth space to squeeze in one line with a sharp-pointed pencil: *6:00, President calls me.*

In a few minutes Amy would know. Meanwhile . . .

She squirmed around in the chair to watch the minutes flick past on the clock.

One thing she didn't understand about the calendar, Amy thought, was that Mother had given it to her. Mother wasn't the kind of person who would buy a magic calendar in the first place. And if she did, she certainly wouldn't give it to Amy.

"Much too dangerous for children to play with," Amy told herself in a stern voice. Then she burst into wild giggles.

Amy was too excited to sit still any longer. She went downstairs. Her mother was at her desk, flipping through a wallpaper book. She glanced up at Amy in that over-the-shoulder way, did a double take, and stared straight at her. Amy remembered guiltily that she should have come down and showed Mother the minute the halo was gone.

"Amy!" Letting the wallpaper book fall shut, Mrs. Sacher sprang at her and took her head in both hands. "It's gone. How did you—"

Shrugging, Amy smiled her sweetest smile.

Her mother looked as if she was going to start lecturing about Amy's career and behaving professionally, but just then the phone rang. "That could be Prue Trenton," said Mrs. Sacher, grabbing it.

Or it could be the president of the United States calling me, thought Amy with a leap of her heart. She glanced at the African mask clock above the fireplace. Just six.

But it wasn't Mrs. Trenton *or* the president of the United States. "Oh, hello, Ursula," said Mrs. Sacher. "To Amy? Well, yes, she's right here." Her mother handed Amy the phone with a puzzled look. "Mrs. McEvoy."

"Oh, Amy." Mrs. McEvoy, Beth's mother, sounded puzzled, too. "I just wanted . . . Was it something Beth told me?" She gave an embarrassed laugh. "I'm feeling a little woozy, and I can't quite remember why I did call you."

Then why don't you hang up, thought Amy, so the president can get through? But she felt she should say something nice to Mrs. McEvoy. "Maybe it was about the play last week," she suggested politely. "Did you think it was good?"

"Oh, yes." Mrs. McEvoy sounded relieved. "Wasn't the play fun? You did so well as Polly. Well, it's been nice talking to you, Amy. Oh! I just remembered something— Could I talk to your mother?"

Mrs. Sacher didn't look pleased to get the phone back. After listening a moment, she said, "I'd simply love to help, but . . . Of course it's important work, but I'm afraid my career doesn't allow . . . All right. I'll think about cochairing a committee."

As she hung up, Mrs. Sacher was frowning. "I suspected I was the one she really wanted to talk to. I *knew* she was going to ask me to head up a P.T.A. committee next fall, and I don't have time for that."

"A committee?" A funny feeling came over Amy.

"Yes," said Mrs. Sacher impatiently, "she's president of the P.T.A. Come on, let's change. It's time for our evening run."

So that was it, thought Amy. P.T.A. president! It just showed that you had to be very, very careful with magic. Every little detail had to be exactly right. She couldn't help smiling, though, at the thought of Mother on a committee with "those dowdy, earnest housewives," as Mother called Mrs. McEvoy and her friends.

After the run it was dinnertime. "Mother," asked Amy as they sat down to their Lean Cuisine dinners, "I was wondering— Where did you get my calendar?"

"Oh, I must have gotten it at Barnes & Noble, when the price went down after Christmas." Her mother spoke absently, but then she frowned. "No. Come to think of it, I *went* to Barnes & Noble to get you a calendar, but they were all very ordinary—cats and rainbows and so on— and I was looking for something special, an accent piece for your room."

"Maybe you got it at the museum," said Amy. She had spent many boring hours hanging around the Museum of Fine Arts shop, waiting for her mother.

Mrs. Sacher speared a piece of broccoli and shook her head again. "No. Actually, I was on my *way* to the museum. I was waiting for a train, when a . . . person came up to me on the platform."

Amy stopped eating, waiting for her mother to go on. But Mrs. Sacher only stared in a puzzled way at the limp green vegetable on her fork. Finally Amy prodded, "What kind of a person?"

"It's hard to believe, but I don't know." Her mother gave a little laugh. "It seems even stranger now that I tell it. She was shorter than me. I didn't get a good look at her face, because she was wearing a cloak with a hood. She came up and tapped me on the arm. At first I thought she was begging for money. But then she took the calendar out of her basket, and I saw that it was for sale."

A short person in a cloak, with a hood! Amy tried to

keep her voice casual as she remarked, "I thought you said never to buy anything from people on the street, because it's usually stolen?"

"That's right," said her mother sternly. "You don't want to encourage people selling stolen goods. But this was different. Who would steal one calendar? No, I was sure that she'd illustrated the calendar herself, and the work was very nice. In fact, I wanted to talk to her about doing some other things for me, but as soon as I paid her for that calendar, she disappeared."

"Disappeared?" asked Amy breathlessly.

"Of course she couldn't have *disappeared.*" Mrs. Sacher chewed her broccoli with sharp movements of her jaw. "I mean, she slipped into the crowd, and I couldn't see where she'd gone. And there wasn't any business name on the calendar—just a logo I haven't been able to trace."

"That's too bad," said Amy. Inside, she was shouting with excitement: "My magic calendar was made for just one person—me!"

"Yes," said her mother. "I could have brought a lot of business her way. That sort of Romantic art makes a perfect contrast to a contemporary room.—Amy, don't try to hide your broccoli under the rice. It has vitamin A and fiber."

Even eating all her broccoli couldn't dampen Amy's spirits. After dinner she skipped upstairs and bounced into her desk chair. Now, to write her own future!

She knew what she wanted, of course: to stay in Rushfield this summer and be in Young Theater with Gretchen and the other kids. But she also knew better than to just write that down on the calendar. Look what had happened about the president calling! Amy smiled to herself. Probably that was how Gretchen had gotten in trouble with magic, from not planning carefully.

All right. So Amy wanted to stay in Rushfield, but she didn't want her mother to get mad at her for not going to Camp KidShine. How could that work? Amy couldn't be in two places at once.

Or could she? After all, this was magic, wasn't it? Magic made impossible things happen.

Yes, two places at once. That was the answer. Then Amy could do what she wanted to do, but her mother couldn't be mad at her, because Amy would also be doing what Mother wanted.

Amy seized the calendar and started to turn to June, so she could write down being in two places at once. Then she hesitated. Careful, careful. Before she wrote herself a whole summer, she had better try out being in two places at once for a short time—say, an hour. Right now. Or maybe in a little while, after she did her homework. Yes, that would be the sensible thing.

There was no more space left in the square with the torn-up, erased paper and the note about the president calling at six, so Amy had to write in the top of the next square. *8:30 to 9:30, Amy in two places at once.*

It was hard for Amy not to watch the clock while she waited for eight thirty to come. She took her math book and work sheet from her book bag and spread them out on the desk, but she couldn't concentrate on the problems.

I could make the time go faster, thought Amy, if I went downstairs and watched television. But, of course, Mother would be working at her desk in a corner of the

41

living room, and she would make Amy go right back upstairs.

Anyway, it would be better for Amy to stay in her room until the magic took effect. There was no way to tell just how the calendar would manage it, and Amy didn't want to upset her mother again.

Finally the numbers on the clock slid up to eight thirty. Amy sat sideways in her chair, clutching the back. She couldn't feel anything.

Eight thirty-one slid by, and eight thirty-two. Amy was only in one place, her desk chair.

Or was she? Amy wondered. What if she were downstairs, too, and didn't know it?

Amy bit her lip. Oh, dear. She had thought she *would* know it, when she was in two places at once. But maybe she should check the rest of the house.

Quickly Amy peeked into her mother's bedroom and bathroom, and into the hall bathroom. She wasn't there. Then with soft steps on the iron stairs, in case another of her was in the living room or kitchen—

But she could see, halfway down the stairs, that she wasn't. Unless she was in the broom closet.

Mrs. Sacher, working at her desk with graph paper and a ruler, glanced up at Amy. "Do you need help with your math?"

Amy shook her head and trudged back up the stairs. What had gone wrong?

Maybe she had already used up all the magic in the calendar, with the stupid halo and that stupid note about the president calling!

Maybe there were certain impossible things that not even a magic calendar could do.

42

Yes, thought Amy a while later, as she climbed into her sleek blond wooden bed. That must be the problem. She would have to figure out some other way for the calendar to help her stay in Rushfield this summer. It *was* impossible to be in two places at once.

5

Two Places at Once

Walking past the golf course the next morning, Amy patted the pocket of her extra-long cardigan sweater. Gretchen's note crackled pleasantly in there. Amy was wondering if she should ask Gretchen's advice about why the calendar hadn't worked last night. Gretchen might not know about magic calendars, but at least she knew *something* about magic. That meant she knew much, much more than anyone else Amy could ask.

But why should that idea make Amy twitch all over? Just now, she had the strangest feeling. As if her body was jerking sideways—in both directions at once.

Hearing giggles behind her, Amy turned and saw two second graders pausing on the sidewalk. They stared at her.

"What's so funny?" snapped Amy. Her voice came out sounding weird—with a kind of echo. Almost like two people talking.

The younger children stopped laughing. They gaped at Amy with bigger and bigger eyes.

And then Amy's body gave one last wrenching jerk—and popped apart like the snap on last year's jeans. I exploded! thought Amy, too scared to scream. I must be dead.

But no. Here she was standing on the sidewalk. Perfectly fine.

Only, who was that standing on the grass a few feet away?

That was Amy, too. Amy 2. There were two of her!

And while Amy 1 was still wearing her short skirt and blouse and extra-long cardigan sweater and socks that matched her sweater and sneakers that matched her skirt, Amy 2 was wearing only her underwear, her watch, and her book bag.

The second graders screamed, pointing. Both Amys screamed, too, at the same time. Then Amy 1 realized that things, bad as they were, were getting even worse. She was being shoved by an invisible force, step by step, into the street. And the second Amy, the one without clothes, was backing slowly onto the golf course. They were being pushed apart.

"It's not fair!" cried Amy 2, stretching out her hand. "Let me have some clothes!"

"I'm sorry," said Amy 1 guiltily, trying to stay on the curb. "I have to go to school. No, wait—here's something extra." She wiggled out of her long sweater.

Amy 2 seemed to be struggling against the force, too, stumbling backward over a golf course sprinkler. "Hurry! Before I'm too far away!"

Just in time, Amy 1 flung the sweater to her other self.

45

Barely catching it by one sleeve, Amy 2 yanked it on and buttoned it with scrambling fingers. Then she whirled around and lunged down the golf cart path, her book bag swinging clumsily.

As the Amy on the sidewalk watched her other self disappear over the seventeenth green, it came to her what had happened. "Two places at once!" she gasped. The calendar magic was working now. And it was working now because Amy had made a stupid mistake: She had meant to be two places at once *last night,* but she had written the instructions in *today's* square on the calendar.

"Go home and erase the calendar!" she shouted to her other self. But Amy 2 was out of sight. She might have heard, and she might not.

A peculiar gurgling sound caught Amy's attention, and she turned back to the second graders. They were gawking at her speechlessly, as if something had knocked the wind out of them. But she could tell they were going to start screaming any minute.

Before they could get out the first scream, Amy bent toward them. "Did you see my sister?" she whispered.

They stared at her without answering. For a moment Amy thought they weren't going to go along with it. Then they nodded, first one and then the other.

"Well, she's a problem child," explained Amy. "Sometimes she goes out in her underwear. My mother's going to send her to a special camp."

One of the younger girls giggled nervously. "Oh," said the other.

"So anyway," said Amy brightly, "we'd better get going to school."

Meanwhile, on the other side of the golf course, Amy

2 raced down the fairway, panting. She spotted a lone golfer in the distance, but luckily no one else was around.

"Change the calendar," she muttered as she ran. Did her other self think she was stupid? Of course she would go home and change the calendar.

Now that she was two places at once, Amy wondered how she could have been so careless, writing in the next square without thinking that the next square was the next *day*. So of course, instead of working at eight thirty last night, the magic had taken effect at eight thirty this morning.

Never mind. Once she got home, she could fix the calendar in a few minutes, thought Amy as she trotted off the golf course, onto Mallard Street. But wait— If Mother had already left, she would have locked the house.

Amy paused in her driveway, gasping for breath. There was a spare key hidden under the deck in back. She was about to go around to the back when she heard a creaking sound, and the garage door started to slide up. Before Amy could get out of sight, the Audi slid out with her mother at the wheel.

Halfway out of the garage, the car stopped with a jerk. Mrs. Sacher jumped out and rushed at her daughter in a whirl of perfume. "Angel! What happened to you?"

"Nothing, really," said Amy. Amazingly, an excuse had popped into her mind. "I had a bet with another girl who liked my clothes. She won the bet, so I had to take them off. Go on, Mother. I'll just run up to my room and—"

"Outrageous!" Reaching into the car, Mrs. Sacher turned off the engine. "This is the most outrageous thing I've ever heard of." She marched Amy through the garage. "I'm going to have to drive you to school, now, and you'll be late even so."

"No, I won't." Amy was sure that her other self was sitting beside Kathy in Room 5A this very moment.

"What did you say?" Mrs. Sacher's footsteps rang below Amy's on the iron staircase. "I'm afraid I know whose idea this bet was. It was that Gretchen Nichols', wasn't it?"

"No!" As a matter of fact, added Amy silently, she tried to talk me out of using magic. "It was a girl in the intermediate school. Someone you don't know."

In her room Amy looked longingly at her desk, where her calendar was propped against the pencil holder. But her mother stood right there with folded arms while Amy put on another outfit: stone-washed jeans, a Hard Rock Cafe sweat shirt, and aerobic shoes.

"Bet or no bet," said Mrs. Sacher, swinging the car out of the driveway, "I want to see all those clothes back in your closet this afternoon. The skirt you were wearing is a Laura Ashley, and the blouse wasn't cheap, either. You tell that girl I'll call her mother if I need to. —Why are you smiling?"

"I'll get my clothes back," promised Amy, straightening her face. She had been thinking that the joke would be on Mother if she called up the mother of the girl who was wearing Amy's clothes. It would serve her right if she had to listen to herself talking for once.

On School Street, as they came up on the half-circle drive in front of the school, Mrs. Sacher flicked on the turn signal. The car started to turn into the drive, but then the steering wheel wrenched out of her grip, and the car straightened and kept going past the entrance.

"Oh, no!" Mrs. Sacher's eyes flashed behind her sunglasses. "Now something's going wrong with the steering. You'd better just get out here. Look how late it is—all the buses have left."

"All right, Mother." Amy hopped out thankfully, swinging her book bag onto her shoulder. She could hide in those bushes after her mother was gone, and wait for the magic to end at nine thirty.

Meanwhile, in the classroom Mrs. Sheppard was taking attendance. Amy 1 sat beside Kathy, bracing herself for the moment when her other self erased the calendar and they joined together again. *If* Amy 2 managed to get home and understood she had to change the calendar.

Kathy's voice broke into her thoughts. "Don't you have one of those new long cardigans that goes with that outfit?"

"Yes, but I had to let her wear it," said Amy absently. "She was so embarrassed."

Kathy stared. "Who was?"

Amy didn't know what to answer, but luckily at that moment Mrs. Sheppard interrupted. "Amy, you pass out the current events work sheets, please. Beth, you may take the lunch orders to the cafeteria. People, I'm still waiting for homework from some of you."

Thankfully Amy jumped from her seat, took the stack of work sheets from the teacher, and began to hand them out. Maybe Mrs. Sheppard wouldn't notice that Amy was one of the "people" who hadn't turned in her homework. She wished she had yelled to Amy 2 to drop the book bag.

At the far side of the room, next to the windows, Amy paused to gaze across the lawn toward School Street. If she could keep an eye on the windows, she could probably see herself coming, just before they joined back together. Room 5A was on the ground floor, but unfortunately there was no way to get outside without going down the hall and out through the front door.

Dennis Boyd stood up in his seat to wave a hand in front of Amy's eyes. "Anybody home? What're you staring at?" Following her gaze toward the street, he exclaimed in a different tone of voice, "Hey! There's a kid in the bushes out there."

He was right. A girl with short blonde hair was sticking her head out of the forsythia bushes, making gestures and mouthing words toward Mrs. Sheppard's room.

Oh, no! That girl was Amy 2.

"Who's that? What's she doing?" Other kids jumped out of their seats and hurried to the windows.

They mustn't see her! Amy 1 let the work sheets drop to the floor and scrambled onto the window ledge. Shaking her head fiercely at Amy 2, she made pushing-down gestures.

"Amy Sacher! What in the world are you doing?" Mrs. Sheppard stalked to the windows and pulled her off the ledge. "People, in your seats, pencils out. You have fifteen minutes to complete your papers. Amy, I'm surprised at you. Look how you let these work sheets get stepped on."

Then there was a chorus of complaints from the boys and girls who didn't have their work sheets yet, mixed with exclamations from Dennis and other kids: "But there's a girl in the bushes, Mrs. Sheppard. Didn't you see that girl?"

"It wasn't a girl." Gretchen spoke in such a determined

voice that Amy stared at her. Gretchen's expression was blank, and she didn't look at Amy. "It was a dog."

"Oh, yeah?" sneered Dennis. "Ever see a blond dog?"

"Yeah, for your information," said Gretchen. "Blond Labrador retrievers. Wise guy."

"People." Mrs. Sheppard sounded as if she were going to start giving out detentions. "Whatever is going on outside, it has nothing to do with us."

That's what you think, said Amy silently. She sank into her chair, clutching a work sheet with a footprint across it. What had happened to Amy 2? She must have gotten home, because she had regular clothes on now. What was the matter with her—why hadn't she changed the calendar?

Kathy nudged Amy. "That wasn't a dog, was it—you were waving at a girl in the bushes. Is she someone you know?"

"Not really," said Amy unhappily. That was the truth. You would think that she would know exactly what her other self was up to, but actually she had no idea. Maybe when Amy 2 had gone home, she couldn't find the calendar—maybe Mother had put it somewhere.

Oh, well, by this time, changing the calendar wouldn't help that much. Amy glanced up at the clock. Nine twenty-three. She had written that she would be in two places at once until nine thirty, so she had only seven more minutes before the magic wore off.

Or did she?

Amy felt cold. What if her other self *had* erased the calendar, but nothing had happened? So far, the calendar had never worked the way she expected. She had *thought* she was going to be two places at once last night, not

52

today. And she had *thought* she would make the president of the United States call her up, but what she got was a call from Mrs. McEvoy, the president of the P.T.A.

What if Amy got stuck being two places at once for the rest of her life? The only good thing about that would be that Mother and Daddy could each have one of her.

Actually, thought Amy with a smile, that *wasn't* the only good thing. Wouldn't it be nice if she could talk to her other self on the phone, and write letters? Like having a twin.

"I see people off in dreamland," said Mrs. Sheppard in a piercing voice, "instead of completing their work sheets."

Meanwhile, Amy 2 crouched in the forsythia bushes along School Street. Had the Amy in the classroom read her lips? Did she understand she should make an excuse to get out of the room before nine thirty? Otherwise, the two Amys would come back together where everyone could see them.

Too bad that some kids had seen *her* when she was waving to Amy 1. Dennis Boyd, Amy thought, and a few others. But at least from this far away, they wouldn't have been able to tell that she was Amy too.

Well, she had done her best. Now there was nothing to do but wait in the bushes until nine thirty. Only four more minutes, thought Amy, looking at her watch. It wasn't so bad sitting here on her book bag, with the sun shining through the green leaves.

Uh-oh. Amy froze as a police car pulled up to the curb near her hiding place. A policeman, a pink-faced man with his stomach bulging over his belt and the back of his neck bulging over his collar, got out. She recognized him—Officer Morello, who came to the school to talk about bicycle safety.

Then Amy noticed something out of the corner of her eye, something much closer than Officer Morello. Something just a few inches from her head. Something with long, waving legs and a fat body. *Eight* long, waving legs.

"Ee! A spider!" Amy popped out of the bushes like toast out of a toaster.

The policeman jumped, too. "Hey, there! Aren't you supposed to be in school?"

"I am in school. I mean . . ." Amy looked around for an escape route, but it was too late to run.

Officer Morello grasped her by the elbow. "Don't get smart with me. Back to your classroom, march."

As the policeman steered her down the drive, Amy smiled. Now, she thought, Officer Morello was going to feel the force that had jogged Mother's car, the invisible force keeping the two Amys in different places.

But no. In fact, Amy was beginning to sense a pull in the direction of the school, like the undertow in the ocean.

"I can go in by myself," said Amy. She tried to pull her arm away as she staggered forward faster. And leaped faster and faster!

"Whoa, there!"

Amy glanced over her shoulder to see the policeman, his stomach bouncing on his belt, leaping after her in giant bounds like an astronaut on the moon.

"Cut that—out!" His voice bounced with his stomach. "You're—going—to be—mighty—sorry!"

In the classroom, Amy 1 felt the pull, too. At first she was glad. It's almost over, she thought. Then she looked around the quiet classroom, with all the kids filling in their current events work sheets. She had better get out of here before it happened right in front of everybody.

Amy raised her hand for permission to go to the rest room, but Mrs. Sheppard frowned and shook her head. "One at a time. Beth is still out of the room. Anyway, you can wait until we finish current events."

Amy bit her lip. It looked like she wasn't teacher's pet anymore. Was she going to have to pretend she had to go to the rest room very bad?

Then Dennis leaped to his feet again, pointing out the window. "There she is! That girl from the bushes! He arrested her."

As other boys and girls scrambled to get a good view, and Mrs. Sheppard followed them to the window, scolding, Amy dropped out of her chair. This was her chance. Pressing her stomach to the floor, she dragged herself along by her elbows, like a prisoner of war crawling under barbed wire.

Then Amy stopped using her elbows, because the invisible force was pulling her along. As if she were lying on a skateboard, she stretched her arms in front of her and scooted alongside the row of desks to the door.

For a moment she thought the door would stop her, because it was hard to push it open from down low. Mrs. Sheppard was herding the class back into their seats, and any minute she would spot Amy, stuck with her hands pressed against the bottom of the door.

Then the door swung open. There stood Beth, her jaw dropping at the sight of Amy on the floor. But before either girl could say anything, the force zipped Amy out the door, between Beth's legs, knocking her over.

Amy tried to scramble to her feet, but now she was going too fast. She zoomed through the hall on her stomach as if she were sledding down a steep hill. At the end of the hall the front door of the school burst open. In flew Amy 2, yanking the policeman after her like a life-size balloon.

Amy 1 rose in the air as if she were swinging on a trapeze, stretching out her hands toward her other self. She had never been so happy to see anyone. Amy 2, smiling eagerly, wrenched her arm out of the policeman's grasp.

From far away, it seemed, Amy 1 heard shouts and footsteps, but she didn't care. Just before her fingertips touched Amy 2's, Amy 1 seemed to hang in the air, like a trapeze at the top of its swing.

And then the two Amys came back together again with a thunderous snap.

6

I Could Help You

"Where's that girl?"

The policeman's voice cleared Amy's whirling head. She—only one of her—was sitting on the floor in the hall.

As Amy looked up, the policeman glared around the crowd of children. "The girl who knocked her down. Did she get away?"

"You should have had handcuffs on her," said Dennis.

"I have no idea where *your* girl went." Mrs. Sheppard reached down and pulled Amy up. "I have enough trouble with this class. Now, people, you march straight back to the classroom," she told them. "Did I *say* to jump out of your seats and run into the hall? I'm not aware of saying anything like that."

But the kids weren't paying much attention to Mrs. Sheppard. They were all staring at Amy.

Amy looked down at herself, and she felt her cheeks

turn red. She was wearing the jeans under her skirt, which had bunched up around her waist, and the sleeves of her sweat shirt hung out of the shorter blouse sleeves. She took a step and almost fell down. No wonder—her yellow sneakers were jammed onto the toes of her aerobic shoes.

"I never thought *she'd* do anything like that," said Beth as she walked off with Gretchen. "Anything that weird."

"Troublemakers always turn up again," said the policeman sternly, loud enough for the kids halfway down the hall to hear. "And they don't get away with their little pranks a second time." He strode off toward the office, clumping the heels of his boots. "I'll be keeping my eyes open, you can bet on that."

Mrs. Sheppard turned to Amy, pushing up her glasses with a sharp poke of her forefinger. "This is the last straw, Amy. Now I'll give you exactly five minutes to go to the rest room and make yourself presentable." She frowned around at the rest of the class. "Everyone else, in your seats *immediately.*"

"I just have to get these extra shoes off so I can walk, all right?" Amy asked the teacher. As she pried her sneakers off the second pair of shoes, she was surprised to catch some sympathetic glances from the kids streaming past her. Dennis even gave her the thumbs-up sign.

When she came back from the rest room, Amy was surprised again, this time by Mrs. Sheppard waiting for her in the hall. "You're really worrying me, you know, Amy. This is the first day you've ever forgotten your homework! And the Amy *I* know has always been so mature and responsible. And polite."

That's because you only knew *one* Amy, thought Amy. But she said, "Oh, my homework. I guess I do have it, after all."

Amy started to unzip her book bag, but Mrs. Sheppard put a hand on her shoulder. "Amy . . . is something troubling you? Maybe there's a certain problem that you just don't know how to cope with."

Amy stared in surprise. How could the teacher know? Then she thought, She doesn't know. All she knows is, I'm acting weird. "No, I'm fine—really. I'm sorry I fooled around." She handed over her homework and ducked into the classroom.

Sinking into her seat once more, Amy suddenly felt tired and shaky. It took a lot out of you, dividing and then merging like that. And she remembered, feeling the sore place on her shoulder, that Beth had accidentally kicked her as she scooted between her legs.

Amy wanted to be quiet for a while, but Kathy started right in. "You know, my sister says in the intermediate school you can't act weird, or else you won't be popular. My sister says nobody wants to be friends with weirdos."

Amy shrugged. "I bet your sister doesn't have very much fun."

Kathy looked offended. She took out her celebrities list, slowly, so that Amy could see what she was doing, and crossed off Amy's name.

What did Kathy think she would do, beg her to put it back on? Amy smiled behind her hand as Kathy pried off the gold stars around Amy's name and carefully put them away in her desk.

Kathy didn't say anything more, but Amy couldn't help

overhearing other kids' remarks and noticing their glances.

"How do you think she did that clothes trick?" one of Dennis's friends asked.

"And I thought she was such a sweet little goody-goody," said someone behind Amy. "Boy, was I wrong!"

"*I* think she's just trying to get attention," put in Beth's sharp voice. "My mother says it isn't good for kids our age to be models, because they start thinking they're really something, and they have a hard time adjusting later."

Amy didn't hear Gretchen say anything, but during lunch Gretchen kept glancing across the table at Amy. Amy couldn't tell what she was feeling, though.

At recess the other girls lined up for jump rope, but Gretchen caught Amy's eye and beckoned, and Amy joined her at the edge of the blacktop. Gretchen looked at Amy, and shook her head, and rolled her eyes. Then she started to laugh. Relieved, Amy laughed, too.

"You're crazy, you really are!" exclaimed Gretchen. "I *told* you not to mess around with you-know-what!" She burst out laughing again. "But you should have seen yourself sitting there on the floor, with all those clothes jammed on."

"Do you know what Mrs. Sheppard said to me in the hall?" Amy sputtered with laughter. "She said, 'The Amy *I* know has always been so mature and responsible'!"

Gretchen thought that was funny, too. " 'Really, Amy,' " she imitated the teacher's voice. " 'Do you think this is mature, hiding your fairy godmother in the bushes?' " Then Gretchen stopped laughing and turned her direct gaze on Amy. "Your wish didn't turn out the way you wanted it to, though, did it?"

"No, no, it's not what you think," said Amy. "I mean, it's not an f.g." Meeting Gretchen's look of disbelief, she added, "You're right, though. It didn't turn out the way I wanted."

Gretchen still looked puzzled. "Maybe I could help you. I mean, of course I don't even know what you're trying to do. . . ."

"I'm trying to stay here this summer so I can be in Young Theater!" Amy burst out. "My mother wants to send me to model camp."

"Model camp? Wow. Why don't you want to go?" asked Gretchen. "That sounds—"

"*You* sound like Kathy," interrupted Amy bitterly. She clasped her hands admiringly and fluttered her eyelashes. " 'Oh, Amy, you're a celebrity.' Just forget the whole thing."

Amy started to turn away, but Gretchen grabbed her arm. "Hey, calm down. *I'm* not going to make you go to model camp. So who *was* that in the bushes, if she wasn't your f.g.?"

Amy took a deep breath. She didn't really want to pick a fight with Gretchen. "Well, I had this idea that I could be two places at once. . . ." But as soon as she started to explain that, she had to backtrack and explain how she had discovered the calendar magic, with the halo.

"I knew it!" exclaimed Gretchen. "I knew something magic was going on when you wouldn't take your hat off. But you know what I thought? I thought it might be a horn, like a unicorn horn!"

Amy giggled. "You mean you thought it was going to poke through my hat any minute?"

"Yeah, I kept watching that hat." Gretchen grinned. Then she looked serious. "When I wrote you that note, I was thinking we could talk after school. But your mother picked you up right away."

"Yes, to go to the photographer's. You should have seen what happened there." Amy told that story, and then she told about the second graders watching while Amy split in two.

"Right there on Mallard Street, in your *underwear?*" Gretchen hooted with laughter, clapping her hand over her mouth. Then an eager expression lit up her face. "Can I come over and see your calendar?"

Amy hesitated. She wanted Gretchen to come over. On the other hand, she was afraid the magic might vanish if she brought someone else in on it. Wasn't it supposed to be just her secret?

"I bet I could help." The bell for the end of recess rang, and Gretchen talked faster. "See, I had all that experience myself, so I know how things can go wrong. I bet I could help you figure out how to make it work right."

"Okay," said Amy. "You mean this afternoon?"

Gretchen nodded. "Like my father says, two heads are better than one." She grinned. "As long as they aren't both your own!"

On the way to Amy's house, after school, she and Gretchen had a lot to talk about. They went back and forth between Gretchen's fairy godmother and Amy's cal-

64

endar, interrupting each other and asking questions and going back to explain from the beginning and jumping ahead to explain what that had to do with what happened later.

Amy was perfectly happy until the moment they turned onto Mallard Street and started to get near her house. She remembered how angry her mother had been this morning, and how she disliked Gretchen. What would Mother say when Amy walked into the house with her?

As they came up the driveway, Amy noticed that the garage door was shut and a strange car was parked in front of it. "I guess my mother has a customer here." That was good—maybe Mother wouldn't pay much attention to Gretchen. Amy led her in the front door.

Sure enough, Mrs. Sacher and a woman wearing a long, trailing scarf were in the living room. Amy's mother was gesturing toward the tall windows overlooking the backyard. "Can't you visualize draperies like this, perhaps in zebra-print velour rather than cheetah? What a dramatic effect!" Then she caught sight of Amy. "Oh, hello, angel." She shot Gretchen a sharp glance as she went on, "I'm glad you got your clothes back."

Nodding, Amy held up her shoes and sweat shirt, rolled up in her jeans. She smiled sweetly at her mother and the customer.

"Hi," said Gretchen cheerfully.

"I'm afraid Amy won't have much time to play this afternoon," said Mrs. Sacher. "Amy, we're going to run up to Filene's as soon as I'm through here—they're having a sale on junior sportswear."

Amy kept the sweet smile on her face, and she kept on

65

walking through the living room and up the stairs. But the afternoon, the best afternoon Amy had had for months, was spoiled. At the top of the stairs Amy spoke in a low voice, looking straight ahead. "I *hate* Filene's!"

"Never mind." Gretchen followed Amy into her room. "Maybe they'll talk for a long time. Where's the calendar?"

The calendar was waiting for them, its picture propped against the pencil holder, the way Amy had left it. "Wow," said Gretchen softly, leaning forward with her palms on the desk. Amy sat down and rested her chin on her hands.

Every time Amy looked at the calendar, the scene seemed more real. How quiet it was in the woods! Very still, but also very much alive. As if the tall trees were breathing.

"Look at that carving," whispered Gretchen, pointing to the stone rim of the pool. Amy wondered why she herself hadn't noticed the carving before. There was an inscription in some mysterious language, and a stone vine twining around the rim, and odd creatures peering out of the vine's leaves.

"But what should I write?" Amy twisted her hands, thinking of her mother downstairs, with the customer who might leave any minute now. "There isn't enough time to think up something good."

"Time." A big smile spread over Gretchen's face. "Hey, if you wrote down that your mother and that lady just kept talking and talking—would that work?"

"Oh—yes! Here—" A bubble of joy rose in Amy's chest, and she reached across Gretchen for the felt pen.

She wrote on the calendar, right under *Two places at once*, *Mother & customer talk until 5:00.* She hesitated, then added P.M.

"Yeah, good thinking," said Gretchen. "What if they talked until five in the morning?" They both snickered.

"But now," said Amy with a sudden frown, "how can we tell if they *will* go on talking?"

The girls tiptoed to the railing in the hall and peered down at the living room. The two women had moved to the sofa, leaning back among the squishy leather pillows that looked like jellyfish. The customer was sipping from a cup.

Gretchen nodded in a pleased way. "Looks good to me."

Amy wasn't sure. "It *looks* good," she whispered back, "but how do we know they're—well, under the spell of the calendar? Maybe they're just having a regular old cup of coffee."

Tiptoeing back toward Amy's room, Gretchen gestured for Amy to follow. "Who cares, as long as they leave us alone? Come on, let's plan how you can get out of going to camp."

7

Two Heads Are
Better Than One

But first Amy wanted to change into comfortable
clothes. Then Gretchen remembered she had to call her
mother and tell her she was at Amy's for the afternoon. So
they went into Mrs. Sacher's bedroom to use the phone.

Once they were there, Amy thought she might as well
show Gretchen some of her mother's most stylish new
dresses, and they tried on some hats in front of the dressing table mirror. Then Gretchen wanted to try some of
the perfume on the dressing table, and they squirted
themselves with three kinds apiece.

Amy had never had so much fun in her mother's room,
although she kept thinking, what if the magic weren't
working after all and Mother suddenly burst in on them?

"We should go check to see what they're doing," she
said, trying to arrange the perfume bottles exactly the
way they had been before.

When the girls leaned over the railing again, Mrs.

Sacher and her customer were still talking. Now Amy's mother was spreading out fabric samples on the coffee table, pointing out this one and that one to the other woman.

"I'm hungry, aren't you?" asked Gretchen. "Why don't we go get a snack? I mean, I don't want to be pushy, since it's your house, but aren't you hungry?"

Alarmed, Amy pointed to the two women on the sofa below.

"They aren't going to bother us," said Gretchen. "Come on."

"But we aren't even sure—" Amy decided it was better not to talk anymore where her mother could hear, and she followed Gretchen down the stairs.

As Amy passed through the living room, trying to look invisible, her mother glanced up from the fabric samples. She sniffed in a puzzled way, and Amy hoped she wouldn't recognize the smells of her own perfumes on Amy and Gretchen. But Mrs. Sacher only said, "Angel, we'll be leaving for Filene's any minute, so you and Gretchen wind up your activities now."

Amy cast Gretchen a despairing look. But Gretchen, already opening the refrigerator, winked. "Can't you see, she's just saying that?" she whispered. "They're under the spell!" She pointed at the clock on the stove. "It's only 4:15." Then her gaze focused on the inside of the refrigerator, and she snorted. "Is this all you have?"

Amy didn't have to look—she knew there was only grapefruit juice, skim milk, seltzer water, and low-calorie salad dressing. She opened a cupboard. "Here's some rye wafers."

"*Rye wafers.*" Gretchen looked in all the cupboards,

shaking her head disbelievingly. "No wonder your mother's so thin. Well, maybe we could make something."

Amy felt nervous about that, since her mother didn't like her to mess up the kitchen. "I don't think so. Anyway, what could we make?"

But Gretchen had already found a little flour and a little sugar and some margarine. After turning on the oven, she started mixing them in a bowl. Amy dug up a handful of stale granola to throw in. "It doesn't make very much dough," she said as she watched Gretchen pat the soft blob out on a square of aluminum foil.

"I wonder if it'll come out all right," said Gretchen. "I've never made just one cookie before."

A couple of minutes later, the kitchen began to smell better than it had smelled since Amy moved here. A few minutes after that, Gretchen pulled the foil, with one large golden brown cookie on it, out of the oven. Amy was afraid they were going too far, carrying the cookie past her mother on their way up to her room. But Mrs. Sacher only said, "I hope you girls didn't leave the kitchen a mess. We'll be taking off for Filene's in three seconds now, Amy." She motioned toward the African mask clock over the fireplace.

"Okay," said Amy cheerfully. This was kind of fun, like walking through a cage of tigers knowing they couldn't hurt you.

"Is that a clock?" asked the other woman, following Mrs. Sacher's glance to the African mask. "Four thirty-five? Is that what it says? I really must be going myself." But she didn't get up from the sofa. As the girls trotted up the stairs, she exclaimed to Amy's mother, "I can't get

70

over your idea to place the TV on a marble column!"

Gretchen nudged Amy from behind, and they both ran snickering into Amy's room.

Putting on an amazed expression, Gretchen flung out both arms and rolled up her eyes. "My dear, I can't get *over* your idea to be in two places at once!"

"Hey, the cookie!" Just in time, Amy caught it as it dropped from Gretchen's hand.

Then they sat on the bed, and Gretchen peeled the foil from the cookie and broke it in half. They gobbled it up. "Mm," said Amy in a satisfied tone, picking a crumb from her skirt. "You're a great cook. —What's the matter?" She turned to follow Gretchen's gaze, which was fixed on the clock by Amy's bed.

It was 4:49.

"How did it get that late?" Gretchen groaned. "I thought we had plenty of time."

They both scrambled to their feet and hurried to Amy's desk.

"Quick, change it to five thirty!" Gretchen reached for the purple pen.

Amy grabbed the pen away. "No, what if it doesn't work? You have to help me with my problem, right now. Hey! I know what." She scribbled on the calendar, *Gretchen helps now.*

Gretchen looked alarmed, and Amy thought she was going to argue. But suddenly she leaned over the desk, her eyes fastened on the calendar picture. "Look at the pool," she whispered.

The pool . . . pool . . . pool echoed in Amy's mind, like ripples. The surface of the dark water quivered. Then the pool smoothed, and slowly a face started to form.

Amy shivered and glanced at Gretchen. Was she seeing the same things Amy saw? She must be, because she looked scared.

The face came clearer. It was framed by wavy ginger-colored hair. Freckles appeared across its nose. It was a girl, a girl with a look on her face as if she wouldn't let anyone tell her what to do.

"That looks like me," muttered Gretchen. She twitched her shoulders, but she didn't take her eyes off the picture.

She *wouldn't* let anyone tell her what to do, either, thought Amy. If Gretchen were me, and she wanted to stay in Rushfield for Young Theater, she'd just tell Mother that. She wouldn't be nervous or change her mind if Mother got mad.

The pool quivered again, and another face formed beside the first. The second face had large brown eyes and short blonde hair.

"That's it!" exclaimed Amy.

Gretchen jerked up from the desk. "What?"

"You *could* tell Mother—only Mother wouldn't know it was you, because you'd look exactly like me." In her excitement, Amy could hardly get the words out fast enough.

"What are you talking about?"

"You're going to switch places with me again, just for a day, and talk to my mother for me."

"No," said Gretchen.

"But look, that's you, in the pool!" Amy pointed. "The pool shows what's supposed to happen."

As the girls watched, the two heads in the pool moved

72

closer, and Amy's head began to slide over Gretchen's, like the moon eclipsing the sun.

"No!" Grabbing the eraser, Gretchen began to scrub at the purple words as if her life depended on it. Amy tried to grab the eraser away, but Gretchen jabbed her with an elbow. The whites of her eyes were showing.

"You *said* you would help," said Amy finally. "Why won't you do it?"

"I do want to help," said Gretchen, straightening up. She seemed much calmer, now that *Gretchen helps* was off the calendar and both faces had faded from the pool. "It's just that—" She looked unhappy. "What if I got stuck being you?"

The words hit Amy like a soccer ball in the head. She stood there stupidly. How could Gretchen say that? That was the worst thing anyone had ever said to her.

"Oh, I don't mean that! Don't look like that." Gretchen seized her arm. "I don't mean I'd hate being you. What I really mean is, it would be so awful not living with your father. And *with* your mother."

That was almost worse. "She isn't exactly *awful,*" said Amy miserably. "It's just that she thinks about my career all the time."

"I'm sorry. Oh, no." Gretchen had turned red. "Don't get mad, all right? Let's just start over again, and try to think of a good idea about what to write on the calendar."

Amy felt a flash of anger. "There's nothing you can do, if you won't switch places."

"All right, have it your way."

"All right, I will."

"All right, good-bye."

"Good-*bye.*"

Amy watched Gretchen disappear through the door, but then she couldn't stand it. "Wait!" She leaped after her.

Gretchen must have felt the same way, because she had stopped right outside Amy's room, and Amy almost bumped into her. But before either of them could say anything, they heard Mrs. Sacher's voice downstairs.

"Good-bye—you'll let me know what you decide, then." The front door closed. Then Amy's mother called, in a piercing tone, "Amy! Down here and in the car, please, right away."

No chance to make up with Gretchen, no chance to write anything else on the calendar. Amy had to go straight downstairs, and Gretchen had to leave.

"Clean this up"—Mrs. Sacher waved at the messy kitchen—"while I get my things together." She started to turn away, sniffed, and frowned. "Who said you could try on my French perfume? Gretchen Nichols, no doubt. We'll discuss this in the car."

But before Amy had finished wiping the flour and sugar off the counter, the phone rang. Amy hoped it might be Gretchen, but Mrs. Sheppard's voice spoke in her ear. "Amy, dear. I—" She sounded nervous. "May I speak to your mother?"

Mrs. Sacher was already standing beside Amy, waiting to see who had called. "Oh, Marilyn," she said into the phone. "I *am* just on my way out, but it's so nice of you to be concerned about Amy." Pause. "I wouldn't call it unusual behavior, the way the other children have been picking on her. For instance, did you know that yesterday someone—I wouldn't be surprised if it was that Gretchen Nichols—tricked her into putting some lights on her head, and they were very difficult to remove, and ruined—"

Amy, sliding the foil wrap into a drawer, ducked her head to hide a smile.

"Pressure?" Her mother's tone was cold. "I can't imagine what you mean. Modeling is everything to Amy. She would never consider what you call 'taking a break.' Yes, of course I know what happened today. Again, if there is insufficient supervision at the school, so that some children are allowed to pick on others— *That's* where the pressure comes from, if you really want to help Amy."

Another pause, and then Mrs. Sacher said icily, "Of course you're entitled to your opinion, and I do appreciate your concern about Amy. Thank you so much for calling."

Her mother hung up, and Amy wiped the counter again, keeping her face blank. So Mrs. Sheppard was worried about her, more worried than Amy had realized. It sounded like she wanted Mother to have Amy stop modeling for a while. That would be nice, if the "while" could be this summer. But Amy was sure Mrs. Sheppard hadn't changed her mother's mind one bit.

"Look at the time!" Mrs. Sacher shook her head at the mask over the fireplace. "Five thirty. Much too late to get to Filene's now. Prue Trenton had better give me the job, after taking up my whole afternoon. I couldn't believe the way she hung around—there really wasn't *that* much to talk about." She turned to Amy. "Angel, go get your sweat suit on."

A few minutes later, jogging along the path around the cranberry bog, Amy found herself staring at the back of her mother's blonde head. She found herself thinking, Look at that branch hanging over the path up there. What if the branch broke off and landed on her head, and Mother forgot all about sending me to Camp KidShine?

Gasping with horror, Amy almost screamed to her mother to watch out. She struggled to run faster, but before she could catch up, Mother was safely past the branch.

Amy fell back into her regular stride, panting. Of course she would never do anything to hurt her mother, even to change her mind.

But as her knees pumped up and down, an idea began to grow in Amy's mind. The idea swelled and shimmered like a soap bubble. What a nitwit she was, trying to talk poor Gretchen into exchanging places with her so she could argue with Mother. The branch idea was silly, too. If Amy wanted to change her mother's mind, she could just *do it herself*—by writing it down on the calendar.

Back home, Amy loped up the iron stairs, two at a time, *clang, clang, clang.* Here comes Amy! Breathlessly she bent over the calendar.

Of course she would make sure the calendar changed her mother's mind without hurting her, thought Amy, picking up the purple pen. There was just enough space left in the square for today, Thursday, for Amy's directions. *6:30, Mother changes mind without hurting herself. Doesn't want me to go to model camp.* She had to cramp the last letters, but she kept them inside the lines for Thursday. She wasn't going to make the same stupid mistake twice.

Raising her eyes to the calendar picture, Amy saw the top of a blonde head glimmering in the dark pool. As she watched, the water in the pool began to bubble, and the image of her mother's head rolled over and over, until Amy shut her eyes to keep from getting dizzy.

8

A Changed Mind

There was something frightening about the sight of that head rolling like a cement mixer, but Amy pushed the feeling away. She had written down *without hurting herself,* hadn't she? Nobody could expect more from her than that.

Sticking the calendar back on the wall, Amy checked the clock. Six thirty-three. She would just go downstairs and see how Mother was getting along.

She found her mother slumped on the living room sofa. One arm was flung over the hand-stitched leather pillows, the ones with fringe like jellyfish tentacles. Mother had often told Amy not to touch those designer pillows, but there she was twisting and tugging the fringe.

"Mother?"

Mrs. Sacher grunted without looking at Amy. Her eyes were fixed on the TV, standing on its fluted column across the room, although the TV wasn't on.

"Mother," said Amy cautiously, "I was just thinking about this summer, you know, about Camp—"

Her mother interrupted her with a louder grunt, and a gesture toward the blank TV screen.

Amy stared at her mother, puzzled. She seemed to want Amy to do something. "You want me to turn on the TV?" She didn't really think it could be that, though. Mother didn't watch much TV, and never before dinner.

But Mrs. Sacher nodded. "Uhn."

Feeling uneasy, Amy pressed the power button. Loud laughter burst out, as if someone had just said the funniest thing in the world. Of course, Mother wouldn't want to watch that sitcom. Amy changed the channel, looking for a news program.

"Hey!" Her mother didn't sit up straight, but her body twitched.

Did she mean to go back to the sitcom? Amy could hardly believe it. But when the taped laughter broke out again, Mrs. Sacher sank back against the sofa cushions with a sigh.

Mother must be stressed out. Having your mind changed was probably a strain, as much of a strain as dividing in two and coming together again. She didn't seem to be hurt, anyway. But just a minute—Amy didn't actually know whether the calendar had done its work. "Mother, do you still want me to go to Camp KidShine this summer?"

No answer. On the TV screen a boy made a smart remark to his mother, and Mrs. Sacher chuckled.

Amy had to repeat the question twice, standing in front of the television the second time, to get her mother's attention.

"Uh-uh." Mrs. Sacher squirmed around on the sofa, trying for a better view of the TV screen.

So the calendar magic had done what Amy wanted. Mother was acting strange, but that was probably normal for someone who had just had her mind changed. Mother would settle down after a while. Well, not settle down. She should perk *up*.

It wasn't quite dinnertime yet, but Amy was hungry. Maybe if Mother had changed her mind about watching TV and making Amy go to camp, she might not care if they had dinner before seven. "I think it would be nice if we had dinner while we watched this show," she said in a loud, bright voice.

Her mother, eyes fixed on the TV, didn't answer.

"I'll fix our dinners now," said Amy in the same bright voice. Her mother showed no sign of interest, so Amy microwaved the frozen dinners and set them on the coffee table in the living room. When kids at school talk about this program tomorrow, I can join in, thought Amy. But, actually, she didn't think the sitcom was nearly as funny as her mother seemed to.

Then Amy did her homework, and her mother watched a detective program. Amy had to write a summary of the last reading assignment, which was about Jeremiah, a pioneer boy who lived on a farm. He had many chores, including feeding the cows and pigs and other animals, and making sure they had straw for bedding. *Jeremiah had a lot of responsibility for his age,* wrote Amy.

Then Amy memorized her spelling list, while her mother watched another sitcom. "Don't you have some business calls to make?" asked Amy uneasily. But her mother only grunted.

Amy took out her science homework and labeled the bones on the drawing of a skeleton. She had to write in what each bone did, too. "Skull—protects the brain." Glancing at her mother, Amy quickly looked away again. The skull wasn't much protection against magic.

"Look, it's bedtime," said Amy with a yawn. Over the fireplace, the mask clock seemed to be yawning, too.

Mrs. Sacher didn't answer. Maybe Amy should just go to bed and leave her on the sofa. No, that didn't seem right.

Wondering if her mother would throw a jellyfish pillow at her, Amy switched off the TV. Mrs. Sacher grunted in protest. "Want to watch that."

"We can't always do what we want to do," said Amy, pulling her up by her arm. "We need our rest so we'll be ready for a good day's work tomorrow."

To her surprise, Mother allowed herself to be dragged off the sofa, led up the stairs, and tucked into bed—with all her clothes except for her shoes still on, but at least she was in bed.

Nobody could expect me to put my mother's nightgown on, Amy told herself as she brushed her teeth. That would be taking even more responsibility than a pioneer kid.

Waking up the next morning, Amy knew right away that she was excited and happy about something but a little worried about something else. She lay in bed for a moment to find out what the somethings were.

Oh, yes! Good news! I don't have to go to Camp Kid-Shine. Amy bounced out of bed, thinking about telling Gretchen. Washing her face in the bathroom, though, Amy remembered the quarrel she and Gretchen had had. She hoped Gretchen wouldn't still be mad at her. They had been going to make up, hadn't they, just before her mother made Gretchen leave?

At the head of the stairs, Amy paused. Now she remembered the something she was worried about, and it wasn't Gretchen. There was no sound of newspaper rustling downstairs, no smell of coffee drifting up from the kitchen. Wasn't Mother up yet? Amy turned and tiptoed into her mother's bedroom.

Under the Chinese silk canopy, her mother was sprawled across the bed. The clock radio that usually sat on the headboard was in a corner on the floor, where it had fallen—or been thrown.

"Mother, it's getting late." Amy poked her in the side, the way her mother sometimes poked her.

Her mother groaned and twitched away from her finger. "Leave me alone."

"Don't you have to go to work today?"

"All right, all *right.*" Mrs. Sacher pushed herself up and sat on the edge of the bed.

There was something different about her face, Amy thought with misgiving. Her mother had the kind of bony face with tight skin that fashion models had. But this morning there was a sort of mushy look around her mouth and eyes. As if something had let go.

"*I'm* getting dressed," said Amy sharply, and left the room.

Later, while Amy was eating her cereal, she saw slippers and the bottom of a robe appear at the top of the stairs. Mrs. Sacher shuffled down with her eyes half shut.

"I made you some coffee," said Amy, but her mother only grunted and slid onto a stool. Amy poured the coffee and set a bowl of Vitaflakes in front of her.

About to leave for school, Amy hesitated and looked at her mother, slumped at the counter. "You'd better get dressed," she warned as she slung her book bag over her shoulder. "You have clients to see, and things like that."

"Don't feel like it," grumbled her mother.

"Don't feel like it!" exclaimed Amy. "Where do you think my career would be, if I just did what I felt like?" On her way out the door, she added, "You're a professional, so start acting like one."

It was satisfying to say those things to her mother. But walking past the golf course, Amy wondered if she should have stuck around until her mother got in the shower. Don't be silly, she thought. I shouldn't have to take care of my own mother. I'm the kid. Mother will have to pull herself together.

At school, Amy was walking down the hall toward Mrs. Sheppard's classroom when she heard quick footsteps behind her. It was Gretchen.

"Hi. Hey, I'm sorry I got mad yesterday."

"That's all right," said Amy. "In fact—"

"I had another idea for what you could write on the calendar," Gretchen went on. "How about—"

"But guess what, I don't have a problem anymore!" Amy felt it had been worth all the trouble she had gone through, to tell Gretchen that. "All I had to do was write down that her mind would change."

85

"That her mind would change," repeated Gretchen slowly. A smile of admiration broke over her face. "Why didn't I think of that? So it worked?"

Amy nodded. "She doesn't care *at all* if I go to camp or not." Of course Mother hadn't seemed to care about anything else, either, but Amy pushed that thought out of her mind.

"Yay!" Gretchen grabbed Amy and danced her around the hall. "You know," she went on more calmly, "it seems like your calendar works a lot better than my—you know, my f.g. did. Maybe we could write some other things down."

"Sure," said Amy. "Anything you want." But she felt another twinge of unease.

During the morning there was a lot of whispering and notes passing back and forth among the girls who were going to sign up for Young Theater tomorrow. Mrs. Sheppard finally lost her temper and made Amy and Kathy and Gretchen and Beth stay in from recess to copy a page from the dictionary. But that didn't bother Amy much.

What bothered her was a picture that kept sneaking back into her mind. The sight of her mother's face, so slack and dull. Probably just a touch of the flu, Amy told herself, although the flu had never slowed down her mother before.

What was Mother doing now? Probably just what she did every morning, after she drank her coffee. Probably Mother had taken a shower and put on one of her business outfits and gone out to work.

It was ridiculous of her to worry about her mother,

Amy told herself, but she couldn't get the nagging question of what Mother was doing out of her head. At lunchtime she went to the school office and made up an excuse for calling home.

Amy waited while the phone rang sixteen times, but there was no answer.

A chill of fear came over Amy. Then she told herself firmly, "No answer means she isn't home, of course." Mother must be out visiting clients and looking at furniture and all those things she usually didn't have enough hours in the day for. Everything was under control.

"Do you want to come over this afternoon?" Gretchen asked Amy as the class lined up for dismissal. "I have to watch my little brother for a while, but after that we could do something."

Amy's cheeks turned warm with pleasure. "That would be fun. I just have to go home first and tell my mother, or leave a note if she isn't there."

"Okay. See you."

A short while later, Amy burst into the front hall of her house, calling, "Mother! I'm home."

She was glad there was no answer. It would be much simpler to leave a note than to explain where she was going, especially since her mother didn't like Gretchen. Besides, if Mother were home, she would probably want to take Amy to that sale at Filene's.

Then Amy paused in the hall, stepping behind the potted ficus tree. Someone was talking. The sound came from around the corner, in the living room, but it wasn't her mother's voice.

In fact, it was a man's voice. "Teresa. Your face has haunted me night and day."

Teresa? Who was Teresa? Her mother's name was Beryl. Cautiously Amy peeked into the living room.

Her mother was lounging on the sofa in her dressing gown, an open pizza box balanced on her stomach.

"Mother!"

Her mother flapped a hand at Amy, but she didn't take her eyes off the screen.

On TV, Teresa said in a quavering voice, "This all seems so—so unreal."

9

Out of Control

Slowly Amy walked over to the sofa and looked down at her mother. There were red pizza stains on the front of her designer dressing robe. Her face looked even mushier than it had this morning. Mother had not pulled herself together.

"I tried to call you at lunchtime," said Amy accusingly. "Why didn't you answer the phone?" As her mother craned her neck her to watch the TV, Amy added, "You can talk to me now. It's just a commercial."

"Driving me crazy. Unplugged it."

Amy followed the nod of her mother's head to the kitchen counter. Sure enough, the phone was not on the wall. It was lying face down next to the note pad and pencils.

"But it might have been people who wanted you to work for them! Or modeling jobs for me."

Her mother shrugged, and the pizza box slid from her stomach onto the floor. "Nuisance."

Amy bit her lip. This was awful. She should do something. But what? Picking up the pizza carton, she stuffed it in the trash. Then she went to the counter and plugged the phone back into the wall. Right away, it rang.

"See?" said Mrs. Sacher. Amy answered the phone.

"Hello, this is Prue Trenton. May I speak to Beryl?"

"Yes," said Amy in the polite tone she used for her mother's customers. "Just a moment, please." She covered the mouthpiece with her hand. "Mother, it's Mrs. Trenton. Maybe she's going to ask you to do her house!" *That* should get Mother up off the sofa. She had been hoping and scheming for this job for several weeks.

But her mother only frowned and flapped her hand as if she were shooing away a mosquito.

Amy's throat began to throb as if her heart were beating there. Mother would rather watch a soap opera than accept an exciting new job from Mrs. Trenton.

Taking her hand away from the mouthpiece, Amy spoke in a choked voice. "My mother—I didn't know she was taking a shower. Is it all right if she calls you when she gets out?"

After she hung up, Amy stood there for a moment. What had she done? Mother wasn't going to call Mrs. Trenton back. She was settled even farther into the jellyfish cushions, their tentacles trailing over her shoulder. She was watching the soap opera with her mouth half open.

No, Mother wouldn't call Mrs. Trenton—unless she changed her mind.

Unless *Amy* changed her mother's mind back.

All Amy's happiness about Gretchen and the Young Theater sign-up tomorrow drained away. She found herself walking across the living room and trudging up the iron staircase. In her room, Amy leaned over her desk to stare at the calendar. *Mother changes mind.*

All she had to do was erase that, and her mother would turn back into her sleek, energetic self. She would put her stained dressing robe in the wash and call Mrs. Trenton and go running with Amy and make dozens more phone calls.

And, of course, she would be absolutely sure that Amy should go to Camp KidShine instead of Young Theater this summer.

Then what earthly good was it to have a magic calendar? "It worked," Gretchen had said. Oh, yes, wonderful, it worked and worked—and Amy wasn't even a little bit closer to getting what she wanted. Amy's hands gripped the back of the chair, and she felt her arms trembling with anger. Her magic calendar was no good to her at all.

Unless— A spark of hope popped in Amy's chest. Maybe she wasn't having enough patience, or paying enough attention. Maybe the calendar itself could give her a better idea. If she sat down and looked into the pool, maybe she would see something.

Letting out a long breath, Amy sank into the chair. And her gaze sank into the picture. Into the silent woods, the clearing with the tree trunks around it like pillars. Amy was there, kneeling by the dark pool across from the cloaked figure.

The image of the pool spread out in Amy's mind, until the pool was a pond . . . a lake . . . She saw nothing but rippling upside-down trees, her own rippling face with big dark eyes, leaning closer, closer, dark water lapping all around, nothing but dark water . . .

Amy was afraid. She had felt like this once last summer at the Delaware shore, floating out beyond the breakers. She had pretended she was out by herself in the middle of the ocean. A little speck in a universe of water. Only now Amy wasn't pretending. She screamed a gurgling scream. "No!"

With a dizzying rush, the picture zoomed back into focus. Amy gave a long, shaky sigh. Then she opened the drawer to find the ink eraser. Breathing hoarsely through her mouth, she began to scrub at the purple letters.

Even though she was back in her room, her feet on the solid wood floor under her desk, Amy couldn't shake off the feeling of floating in that terrible, vast water. Alone. The feeling made her want to shout for a lifeguard: Help!

The ink had soaked through so far that the eraser rubbed a hole in the thick paper, but at last every trace of purple was gone. Amy straightened her stiff back, pushed the chair out from the desk, and hurried to the head of the stairs. There she paused, hearing her mother talking on the phone below.

"—phone was out of order *all day,* can you believe that? Of course I'm thrilled you decided to go with my interior design plan. . . ."

Mother didn't sound exactly *thrilled,* thought Amy. She sounded pleased with herself, and maybe as if she thought Mrs. Trenton was the one who should be thrilled to have Beryl Sacher for an interior designer. Amy peered over the railing.

Standing at the counter as she talked on the phone, her

mother held her back as straight as a dancer's. Her shoulders were turned a little, and one hand was on her hip. Amy couldn't see much of her face, but she was sure it wasn't mushy any more.

Well, fine, thought Amy dully as she walked back to her room. Mother's mind is changed back. But what about me? She hesitated a moment at her desk. Maybe she would rip the useless magic calendar to pieces. Instead, she picked up the pen and wrote slowly, *Help.*

That was silly. Who was going to help? Mrs. Sheppard already tried. Amy couldn't think of anyone else who would want to help her. Daddy could if he wanted to, but he had planned with Mother to send her to camp.

Amy was tired. In fact, she felt as mushy as Mother had looked a few minutes ago. She flopped onto her bed and lay there on her back, staring at the blank ceiling.

Gretchen might have helped, if she had been willing to switch places with Amy. She might have changed her mother's mind the right way—just that one little bit of her mind about Amy going to camp.

Amy closed her eyes. If I weren't such a wimp, she thought, I'd stand up to Mother for myself. If I were like Gretchen, I'd just march downstairs and stand in front of her and say, "Look here, Mother. I'm not going to camp. I'm staying here and taking Young Theater, and that's that."

A strange tingling came over Amy, and her eyes popped open. She felt embarrassed and excited at the same time. What an idiot she was! That's the way she should have used her magic calendar in the first place. Amy didn't need Gretchen to speak up for her. Because if she wrote down on her calendar that *she* would talk her mother into letting her stay in Rushfield this summer, she could do it herself.

Swinging her legs over the side of the bed, Amy bounced up. Could it really happen? Mother's meek little angel, standing up for herself?

The idea made Amy giddy, and a giggle bubbled up in her throat as she pattered down the stairs. She hoped she wouldn't have to wait. No, Mother was just hanging up the phone.

"Well! I *thought* the Trentons were going to hire me," said Mrs. Sacher in a satisfied tone. "I can usually tell. Angel, go get your running clothes on."

"I wish you'd call me 'Amy,' not 'angel,'" said Amy. She couldn't help smiling at the surprised look on her mother's face. "And there's something I want to talk about."

Mrs. Sacher's mouth tightened with impatience, but she said, "All right." She glanced at the clock. "We can take a few minutes. What did you want to talk about?"

Amy's heart started to pound. But she knew she could say what she wanted to say, with the power of the calendar behind her. "I don't want to go to Camp KidShine. I want to stay in Rushfield this summer and be in Young Theater."

Her mother's eyebrows drew together as she gave a little laugh. "We discussed this before, angel. Don't be ridiculous. You've been accepted at the camp, and I've paid the deposit, and there's nothing more to talk about."

"I don't want to go," repeated Amy.

Sitting on the stool, her mother began to swing one leg, like an irritated cat switching its tail. "I think I'm beginning to understand something. Is this why you've been acting so strange? First pulling that silly stunt with the lights in your hair, and then betting away your clothes, then stuffing yourself with junk food? Don't shake your head no, because I found the pizza box in the trash."

"I didn't—" Amy began.

But her mother interrupted. "All right, just tell me this. What's so important about being in the theater program?"

"Because my friends are in it!" Amy burst out. "Because I don't *want* to go off to camp where I won't know anybody, all over again! I hate that!" She was trembling, but she felt wonderful. At last the calendar was doing her some real good.

Mrs. Sacher gave a scornful jerk of her head. "You have to make a few sacrifices if you want a career, of course. I don't know if you realize how much of my social life I've given up to manage your modeling."

"But the theater program would be good for my modeling." Amy was surprised when this reason popped into her mind, but she also knew it was true. "Tina—you know, that teenage model I met on my last job—she said acting experience would help me loosen up. She said—"

"Yes, I'm sure Tina said a lot." Mrs. Sacher snorted. "She thought she was quite the expert. I don't care to listen to all Tina's opinions, however. But I'm glad we got this out in the open," she went on briskly. "I hope that's the end of this talk about not going to camp, and the end of your uncooperative behavior. Now let's change and go running."

Her mother left without waiting for an answer. As her firm clanging footsteps sounded on the stairs, Amy stood at the counter, shocked. What had gone wrong? She had felt so good just now, she was sure she was going to change her mother's mind. Wasn't the calendar working anymore?

Amy trudged up the stairs after her mother, still stunned. In her room she leaned over the desk, staring reproachfully at the calendar. "Why didn't you do what I wrote down?"

Then she saw, with another shock, that there was only one thing written in today's square: *Help.* In the calendar picture, there was something floating in the dark pool—a bottle, like a Coke bottle, with a message inside.

So I didn't write down anything about me talking my mother into letting me be in Young Theater, thought Amy. I *thought* about doing it, but I didn't do it.

To Amy's surprise, she felt a smile spreading over her face. Amy, you nitwit! You thought it was the calendar making you stand up to Mother, but it wasn't. It was you! Just you!

That means, Amy's mind raced on, if I write it on the calendar, Mother will have to change her mind.

Breathing fast with excitement, Amy seized the pen. But then a movement outside the window caught her eye, and she hesitated. What *was* that?

Still holding the pen, Amy went up to the window. Someone was striding toward the house from the pine trees at the edge of the backyard. Someone wearing a long cloak with a hood, in spite of the mild weather, and carrying a basket on her arm.

Amy felt a chill herself, watching the someone walk toward her house. The cloak rippled with her even steps, not fast and not slow, as regular as a clock ticking.

96

10

Who Needs Magic?

It's the person on my calendar, thought Amy. A shiver wiggled down her spine. What does she want?

Watching the cloaked figure walk across the lawn, not slow, not fast, Amy remembered her mother's story. She had gotten the calendar from someone who looked like this. Now the same person had appeared, because—why?

To take back the calendar.

"No!" cried Amy, as if the hooded person could hear her. Oh, it wasn't fair. Just when she needed help the most, she had found out she had a magic calendar. And now, just as she was finally going to use it to get her wish, she had to give it up.

Amy *had* to give it back. Somehow she knew that her time was up, that there was no way to get out of it. Amy might as well dig in her heels and lean back to keep the earth from turning as try to hold on to the calendar.

With steps as measured as the cloaked figure's, Amy fetched the calendar from her desk and walked down the stairs and out the sliding door to the deck.

The person with the hidden face waited on the lawn below the deck. She didn't speak, but she held up her hand.

For a second Amy had a wild thought of tearing out that one page, the picture of the pool in the forest. But of course she couldn't do that. She had to give back the whole calendar. Amy leaned over the deck railing, stretching out her hand.

The figure below reached up, still keeping the hood well over her face. Then Amy let go, and the spiral-bound pages flapped down.

Amy thought it would be hard to catch the calendar with the pages flapping, but the calendar folded itself in midair and slipped into the waiting hand. Then, while Amy blinked, it was tucked out of sight in the basket. The cloak swirled as the mysterious person turned. And again the cloak flowed and rippled as she walked across the lawn and through the trees with measured steps, finally vanishing among the dark, feathery branches of the pines.

Amy might have stood on the deck for a long time, staring at the place where she had last seen the cloaked figure. But the phone began to ring. Amy went into the kitchen and picked it up.

"Amy," said a man's voice. "How's it going?"

"Daddy." Amy was surprised—he usually called on Sundays. "Hi. Er—fine."

"Are you sure?" Before Amy could answer, her father went on. "I had the funniest feeling a little while ago. In

fact, it wasn't just a feeling. It was a picture in my mind, like a dream except I was awake. I saw a bottle floating in water, with a message in your handwriting." He paused.

"What was the message?" whispered Amy.

"Well—" He gave an embarrassed laugh. "It was 'Help.'"

"Oh, Daddy." A huge sob burst out of Amy's throat. She could hardly speak. "Don't make me go to camp. Please let me stay here this summer! Please!"

"Sh, sh, sweetheart. Calm down. Tell me what's the matter."

Her father's kind voice made Amy cry even harder. But finally she quieted down enough to explain, between sobs and hiccups, how much she wanted to be in Young Theater with her friends, and how much she didn't want to go to model camp with a bunch of kids she didn't even know.

When she had finished, her father said, "I don't blame you. Let me talk to Beryl about this."

"Okay." Sniffling, Amy drew a shuddering breath. "But—you won't get her mad, will you? I can't stand it when she starts screaming."

There was a silence on the other end before her father answered. "Poor Amy. It hasn't been very nice for you, has it, listening to your mother and me slugging it out. But don't worry, I know how to handle her on this one."

Hearing footsteps, Amy glanced over her shoulder. Her mother, in her sweat suit and headband, was striding across the living room. "Okay," she said shakily. "Here she is." To her mother she said, "It's Daddy."

Amy was afraid to hang around and listen, but she was more afraid to go off and not listen. She walked around the living room a couple of times, and she went out on the deck and came back, and she climbed halfway up the stairs.

At first Mrs. Sacher's face was stony as she listened to Amy's father. Amy heard her say, "Chances like this don't come along every day, you know, and if she throws it away . . ."

But gradually her mother's expression became thoughtful, and the scraps of conversation Amy caught took on a different tone. ". . . needs to loosen up, and acting lessons would help . . . of course you wouldn't know this, but she's been showing some stress lately—her teacher called about it . . . needs stability . . ." Then, in a final-sounding voice, "I'm glad you agree with me, then. Of course you understand you won't get back the deposit for the camp. Fine. I'll explain to Amy."

Mrs. Sacher hung up and called across the living room, where Amy was clutching the iron railing. "Well, I'm afraid Camp KidShine is out for this summer, Amy. Your father had to agree with me that you need to spend the summer at home. It's obvious from your behavior that I need to keep a close eye on you, and anyway the Rushfield theater program will help you loosen up in your modeling."

Amy felt her heart lift. "I—I think so, too."

The phone rang again. Mrs. Sacher started to reach for it, then gave an impatient wave of her hand and hurried to the front door. "I'm going running. Take a message."

But it wasn't for Mother; it was Gretchen. "Why didn't

you come over? It's going to be almost dinnertime, if you don't hurry."

"I had to do something else first," said Amy. She couldn't possibly explain over the phone. "But I'm through, now."

"Well, come over. I don't have to watch Jason anymore, so we could go somewhere."

"How about the stationery store?" asked Amy. "I have to get a calendar."

The next morning the high school gym was crowded. Each of the programs in the Recreation Department had a different table along the wall, and there was already a line for Young Theater. "Come on," Amy urged her mother, "before it gets filled up."

A few places ahead of them, Gretchen leaned out of line to wave at Amy. "Did you see that sign?"

"What sign?" Amy called back. Then she looked up where Gretchen was pointing, to the wall under the gym clock. There was a long banner with rainbow-colored letters: A SUMMER OF MAGIC.

Amy grinned at Gretchen. "Who needs it?"